T0151798

THE BOOK OF EMOTIONS

THE BOOK OF EMOTIONS
JOÃO ALMINO

translated by Elizabeth Jackson

Dalkey Archive Press
Champaign : : Dublin : : London

Originally published in Portuguese as *O livro das Emoções* by Editora Record, Rio de Janeiro, 2008
Copyright © 2008 by João Almino
Translation copyright © 2011 by Elizabeth Jackson

First edition, 2011

Library of Congress Cataloging-in-Publication Data

Almino, João.
[Livro das emoções. English]
The book of emotions / João Almino ; translated by Elizabeth Jackson. -- 1st ed.
p. cm.
ISBN 978-1-56478-681-4 (acid-free paper)
I. Jackson, Elizabeth (Elizabeth Anne), 1955- II. Title.
PQ9698.1.L58L5813 2011
869.3'42--dc23
2011028548

Partially funded by a grant from the Illinois Arts Council, a state agency, and by the University of Illinois at Urbana-Champaign

Obra publicada com o apoio do Ministério da Cultura do Brasil / Fundação Biblioteca Nacional / Coordenadoria Geral do Livro e da Leitura

This work published with the support of Brazil's Ministry of Culture / National Library Foundation / Coordinator General of the Book and Reading

www.dalkeyarchive.com

Cover: design and composition by Danielle Dutton, illustration by Nicholas Motte
Printed on permanent/durable acid-free paper and bound in the United States of America

"So the remembered world's

songs and flooded paths
This heap of photographs"

—Michael Palmer

I had the habit of carrying a camera over my shoulder to record whatever crossed my path, like a writer taking notes, a forgetful historian who wanted to leave a statement, or a scientist making an inventory of the world. To photograph is to see with a trained eye, to crop and keep what one sees. Upon taking the picture, the photographs became engraved in my mind, like mirrors of what I once was. They are eternal instants, frozen in a personal museum.

I shall open this museum. It will be my legacy, though with this decision I'm not announcing that I'm about to die. Death hovers around old people like me, but it likes surprises. It came near many times without my knowing it at the time. Now, to keep it at bay, all I'd have to do is sell myself to science and then exchange my old organs for new ones. They say that I could even recover my eyesight. I stubbornly insist on remaining a natural being, like wormy organic apples that rot more easily. There are those who prefer them to apples treated with radiation to keep beautiful and shiny for weeks on end.

When I left Joana and Rio de Janeiro two decades ago, I kept a photographic diary for a little over a year. It's the most personal thing in my files. But time has rid me of its sentimental, complaining style. Now, it evokes in me drier, more realistic interpretations. But I still remember it, page after page, because each one of them exhales feelings. Those photographs reveal themselves in rich detail in my memory, even more than if it were possible to see them. They're like Stieglitz clouds; each one equals an emotion. My blindness reveals their essence, for in the end, to best see a photograph, you have to close your eyes.

The idea of using this diary as the basis for writing my book came to me while talking today to my goddaughter Carolina. She spent the entire morning here and brought me a version of Clarice Lispector's stories on Brasília that I could listen to on my computer.

– Godfather, if you won the lottery, what would you do with the money? she asked me with the sweet voice that reminds me of her mother's.

– Me? Nothing. If I could see, I would watch films and more films and I would start taking photographs again.

My blindness keeps me from seeing Carolina. But it's as if I could see her. Her voice updates the face and body of the child I saw growing up. She would have the same dark, straight hair; the same clever, dark eyes; the same fair complexion.

– Don't you want to organize your files?

When a girl of twenty poses such a question to an old man of seventy, she could easily word it as a threat, which Carolina didn't do out of politeness, but even so, I heard: "If there is anything of any value in this infinity of boxes and computer files, it would be better for you to sort it out before you die, otherwise, it's destined for the trash." My files are now roughly sorted into landscapes, portraits, nudes, photos of former President Paulo Antonio Fernandes and of Vila Paulo Antonio, and other themes of lesser importance.

Carolina is capable of digitizing whatever I need and of reordering my files on the computer. I was the one who created her interest in computers, as her mother once told me.

– Godfather, I have a friend who wants to be a photographer. She admires your work and she's looking for an internship. It would be amazing if she could have access to your files.

I asked her to describe her friend.

– She's dark . . . She sings. Plays the guitar . . . She's twenty-five.

June 8, morning
In the midst of the dry season, there was a downpour, perhaps the last rain before the long drought.

I listened to Clarice's story on the computer. In one passage, she defines the people of Brasília, the Brasiliarians:

> Brasília is from a splendorous past that no longer exists. This kind of civilization disappeared millennia ago. In the fourth century B.C., it was inhabited by extremely tall, blond men and women who were neither Americans nor Swedes and who sparkled in the sun. They were all blind. . . The more beautiful the Brasiliarians were the more blind they were, the more pure and the more they shone, and the fewer children they had. The Brasiliarians lived about three hundred years.

I imagined that if I could live three hundred years and had not fathered a child, I would be the reincarnation of a Brasiliarian.

June 9

I mentioned to Mauricio my plan to make new use of the photo-graphic diary.

– Why don't you record your comments about the photographs? Then we can get someone to compile them into a book.

– I want to reflect, to develop my ideas.

– That'll only get in the way. Get right to the point. Say what you want and show the photos. No one has time to think.

Mauricio told me that his whole right arm is tattooed. He had me touch the two studs in his ears and the gold ring in his nose. He has become a tall, corpulent man, even taller than I am. He reminds me of who I once was in my youth, and not just because of the studs, but mainly because of the unfinished years of education, changing from one major to another. And the love I have for photography he has for music, but not classical music, which is Carolina's passion. He's heir to the old Brasília rockers and composes in a beat called rockonfusion.

June 10

I'm not going to follow Mauricio's advice. I won't ask anyone to write for me. If Homer, blind like me, was able to compose the Iliad *and the* Odyssey, *why wouldn't I be capable of writing my own per-sonal little odyssey? I enjoy hearing the phonemes of each letter and this computer's calming voice, which I can modulate according to my mood by using this program for the blind. If necessary, I can also listen to my texts on the talking camera. I'll only need assis-tance selecting and reordering the photographs in my old diary, the photographic diary. Aside from that, I still find it complicated to reorder my texts relying only on my hearing. No matter. I'll make a minimum of revisions and keep the paragraphs in the order that they come to mind.*

Saint John's Night, 2 o'clock in the morning
Both in the book I intend to write and in this new diary, I'll comment on whatever comes to mind, in the order it comes to mind. For example, just now—and out of order—my dog Marcela came to mind. There are days when she is the only one around me, that is, if I don't count the delivery man who brings meals to me. She's a patient, honey-colored Labrador who lives with me on the third floor of a building at 213 North. She guides me from one place to another, and when she isn't guiding me, she stays at my feet. She barks at other dogs passing by, and today, she barks at fireworks, the sound of children, the Northeastern music, and the Saint John's Day square dancing. The dancing is lively; I've been listening to the sounds of the triangle and the accordion, visualizing the colorful flags fluttering in the wind, and I'm unable to sleep.

June 26
It wasn't hard learning to live alone. I fill the time between the visit of one friend and another with my writing. Since friends are few and almost never visit, I have plenty of time to fill. Aside from those who left Brasília, I have already lost the friends from my generation. My friends' children and a few friendships made in recent years are all that remain. To strip truth to its essence, the only one who remains, besides Mauricio, is my goddaughter Carolina.

I thought about beginning the book with portraits of them. But that would invert the order of the story. Mauricio and Carolina should not take precedence over their parents. Or more precisely, over their mothers.

Still June 26, 10 PM

Reflecting on what I wrote above, I should confess that on one point I wasn't quite truthful. Being alone is not always easy. To be exact, there are days in which I transport myself to that tree in the film Amarcord *and there, perched on the highest branch, shout over and over:* "Voglio una donna! Voglio una donna! Voglio una donnaaa!" *Sometimes I see myself as Tiresias, punished with blindness for having seen Athena naked. I saw her nude and not just once, but several times, until she finally decided to cover my eyes with her hands. The goddess was unable to restore my sight, but in exchange she gave me the ability to use writing as the means to ground memory. I know that this gift should be enough for me, since the old must live only from their memories. But a friendly smile, a tender hand, a voice that reads me a page of a good book, and a companion for a stroll around City Park or the nearby Water Hole Park would give a nobler meaning to my existence.*

Besides, vicarious love fills some of love's emptiness in me. I do what I can for Mauricio and Carolina to end up together. They're obviously fond of each other. With a little push, which I won't fail to give, they'll fall into each others' arms.

June 27

The book I intend to write, based on my old photographic diary, could be considered a scrapbook of my incomplete, sentimental memories from a period in which I could see, and saw too much.

I will call it The Book of Emotions. *Life is not measured in minutes, and memories are not written to enumerate everything that happens in a chronological order, as if measured by the hands of a watch. As a matter of fact, I wear a watch without hands. Like the buttons on a radio that skip right to the stations with the best reception, my memory jumps to things that can still make my heart beat. Parodying the poet, I blindly penetrate into the realm of images.*

June 28
Today, Mauricio helped me select five of the photographs to guide me through the beginning of the book. It's not worth using all of the photos from the old diary, and I'm thinking of adding some that aren't there. The basis for my selection will be the emotion I felt when I took the photograph, was photographed, or looked at a photograph.

June 28, after the 8 PM soap opera
The idea for The Book of Emotions *is that the person speaking will not be me but rather another Cadu, someone twenty years younger who can see and who composes a photographic diary. It's a way of discarding my cane and my slow, tired manner of walking. He sits down beside me and begins to speak to me. He carries a box full of photographs that he begins to show me, one by one.*

June 29
Now that the first photos have been chosen, all I need is the desire to begin writing.

1. Geometry of doubt

When Joana and I discovered that we couldn't have children, we didn't undergo the tests to determine whose problem it was. That impossibility was a blessing: we didn't want to have children. However, it was unlikely the infertility was mine because many years before in Brasília another woman had conceived my child.

We tried living only for pleasure and disengaging ourselves from day-to-day obligations, problems, and cares. We believed we could avoid jealousies and recriminations, as well as the duty of fidelity, the other side of adultery. I had the romantic illusion that living in separate quarters from Joana would make us feel like eternal sweethearts, single and childless. Separated by only a few floors, it's true. After my first wife's suicide, and ever since Joana had divorced, we'd decided to live in the same building in Flamengo.

She was the owner of both apartments. She'd inherited a publicity company from her father, managed by one of her brothers. She could live off the income if she wanted. But once in a while she wanted to prove her usefulness and pose as an entrepreneur helping her brother. And her passion for fashion had led her to open a store and create the "Joana Rodrigues" line.

It was February, 2001, and I was in my fifties. With age, who doesn't tend toward the ridiculous? Each person contributes his own dose of stupidity to the stupidity of the world. Millions of men on a night like that one, in that same city of Rio de Janeiro, looked at the woman beside them and asked themselves if she still felt the same desire for him. If she still loved him. If she was interested in someone else. But not all of them ran the risk, as I did,

14

of falling from the ninth floor, to take photograph # 1 (see above). It's a photograph of the façade of a building from the 1950s taken from above looking down. The photograph is geometric in its composition, defined by the edges of the illuminated windows on several floors and by the arrangement of people at the entrance. From the distance of nine floors, several small heads can be seen, arranged as if on a chessboard, each facing in the same direction. The pavement shines in the background, reflecting the streetlight. One person, exactly in the center, looks up. It's a middle-aged man, balding with light-colored hair. A driver holds the door of the luxury car open behind him.

I have hundreds of similar photographs, but that is the only one from a strange angle, in which the entire building façade, from my floor to the ground, appears. I was so interested in what was going on down below that I leaned out the window with the camera to take the photograph. I had purchased a refracting lens that let me take pictures, without being noticed, of things off to the sides. I had used that lens to photograph spontaneous expressions of people on the street, at bus stops, at subway exits, in Cinelândia and even at an entrance to the Rocinha slum. Now I'd decided to focus the camera for an entire week at the window with the lens turned down, and through the viewfinder I spotted men entering the building with suspicious looks on their faces—for example, a hopeful smile. I ignored the ugly, the old, and the paunchy ones. Joana wouldn't be interested in those. I had forgotten the category of the ugly rich, the very rich, until on that night I recognized the far-off tiny face of Eduardo Kaufman looking in the direction of my camera, as though he were only a *detail to fill that photograph.*

It's not a photograph to be appreciated for its aesthetic qualities or for the information it communicates. Looking at it, I'm like a poet who cries when reading his pathetic love poem and feels the very body of his loved one's pulse in the verses, although he's aware that the very same poem may appear dull to other readers. Or else like the author of an autobiographical novel who, after exposing so much about himself and writing with so much emotion, knows that his emotion doesn't move those annoyed by a story with no plot. As a matter of fact, the impartial observer notices neither the courage nor the despair present in that photograph. Each picture is different depending on who's looking at it. After I snapped the shutter I waited twenty minutes and went up to Joana's apartment.

[June 29, night]

2. The man who saw too much

I filled my lungs, preparing to fire words like bullets at Joana and Eduardo, but I was prevented by my own timidity. Instead, I filled the silence with imaginary conversations between the two of them. With their conversations about *me*. This time Eduardo didn't brag about politics and business. He proposed marriage to Joana. She accepted when presented with the diamond ring he pulled from the inside pocket of his jacket. He took her to São Paulo. And there, Joana came increasingly to admire Eduardo's qualities, refined by money. She planned to have a fertility treatment and then children, lamenting the years lost at the side of a vulgar, immature man like me.

– Eduardo just asked about you, Joana said, with the same husky voice that always charmed me.

I barely heard what Eduardo was saying. I noticed only the arrogance of someone who believes himself king of the world and of Joana.

– I want to make you a proposal, he said. To send you to Brasília, all expenses paid. I need a photographer for a project about Paulo Antonio.

When still young, more than thirty years before, I had lived in Brasília with the sister of the then President Paulo Antonio Fernandes and had many of the photographs on the front page of the *Correio Braziliense*.

Eduardo wanted to get me as far away from Joana as possible. I'd never agree to that, nor would I ever leave her apartment before Eduardo himself left. I had always picked fights with him. If necessary, I'd smash his face in.

– Your material is quite valuable; you just don't realize it. No other photographer had as much access to Paulo Antonio's private life.

Unlike today, my problem was seeing too much. I saw everything going on around me down to the smallest details. The visible was real and the real was visible. To know and to see were the same thing. What I couldn't see probably didn't exist. At that moment I saw, but it would have been better not to have seen. Not to have seen Joana, not to have seen Eduardo Kaufman. I looked away, but Joana's bare shoulders danced to the movement of Eduardo's hands. I captured that dance with my camera through the reflection in the window. Photo # 2 (above) doesn't allow me to lie: I was present, watching that dance. It provided me with the evidence I needed. It was like the proof of a crime. Afterward it reminded me how Joana had grown even more seductive with age. We see her thin profile, the perfection of her nose and the volume of her breasts. Her hair, long and blonde when I met her, was short and had regained its natural color, a light chestnut, adding gravity to her aquiline gaze. Photography is neither a part of a film nor a moment in a sequence of facts. It's a time for reflection, observation, and discovery. Looking at a photograph, it's possible to close one's eyes, not to stop seeing, but rather to see more. That's why it's not surprising that although I'm blind I can still see the photograph of Joana and Eduardo Kaufman—and see it better—with its reflections and superimposed planes that also make it the photograph of a nightmare.

June 29, night

Enough for today. It's already midnight, and I've made it a habit not to go to bed after eleven. I've been rising early and tomorrow I'll continue.

In the late afternoon Carolina called me to find out when she can bring her friend. We agreed on five days from now.

July 1

I won't be able to move forward with the book. For the past two days I haven't stopped thinking about Eduardo Kaufman, which paralyzes me. I have to decide. Either I forget about him and am brief in my comments about him, or else the whole book will be about that bastard and his bastardy. A contemptible person doesn't deserve a book. One possibility is to restrict myself to the photographs, abandoning words entirely. I think of photography as an infinite alphabet of images that creates a visual language of the world.

3. Evening at seaside

I couldn't understand why Joana was interested in a jerk. Just because he was rich, filthy rich? Arrogantly rich. He thought money bought everything. A rich man pretending to be generous. I wasn't going to give up Joana. And I wouldn't let on about my jealousy of that disgusting nobody. I knew Joana; she'd announce it to half the world as if it were extremely funny and totally absurd.

An intense reciprocal sexual desire had brought us together. We had never spoken of love or marriage. A lack of romanticism? Perhaps. But we had needed each other, we felt pleasure being together, and why couldn't the heart be the spring for that river of desire? Now that her desire had ceased, and so I wouldn't lose her, I imagined that her elusive if not unreachable heart would be receptive to an engagement ring. I remembered the word "epiphany" that I'd heard at Mass when I was a child in Porto Alegre. Over time I came to learn its meanings, of sublime, transcendental, divine manifestation. That word gave a flavor of nobility to my pedestrian mind, softened my coarse character, and made me feel like a superior person, detached from my carnal vulgarities.

– It doesn't help. You're selfish. You think only of this. You never gave me any affection, Joana told me when she refused the ring. In fact it wasn't an impressive piece of jewelry. The band was narrow, made of a small amount of cheap gold. I should have predicted that to melt Joana, the affection would need weight and many carats.

– This what? I knelt and tried to kiss her feet.

– Don't be ridiculous. Now that you can't get any other woman you come bother me.

– I've had it. You'll never see me again, I threatened. Out of vanity, I should have initiated our break-up. I didn't want to go through the humiliation of being abandoned by her. Most of all I didn't want to hear it confirmed that she'd leave me for Eduardo Kaufman. I'd thought that we wouldn't reach such extremes. My threat would make her regret what she'd just said.

– It's all over. And what's more, I'll need the apartment. Get out, she screamed, furious.

Joana was determined to throw me out of the building and out of her life over some tacky, tawdry drama.

Night fell, relentlessly, without pity or forgiveness, slowly killing me like some indifferent, calculating assassin. I awoke in the middle of the night in a cold sweat. An entire life, marked by impermanence and instability, weighed me down. I didn't want to be an Eduardo Kaufman, but I wanted to be myself even less. I should have accumulated diplomas, saved money. At least I could have started sooner to pay into a pension fund that would give me financial security when I could no longer make a living from my photography.

My problem was that other people considered me a mediocre photographer and had no sense of the great artist living inside me. And Joana, taking me for a vulgar man, was incapable of seeing the great lover in me. The thing was I couldn't forget Eduardo Kaufman. A worse problem tormenting me that night was that I was thinking about calling him to accept the job offer.

Ironically, people sometimes said to me, "You really are an artist." And I felt like an artist when at four in the morning I set out my few items of clothing, my photographic equipment and my laptop; when I packed my bag, looked at my empty wallet and foresaw hunger, illness and decadence. I felt like an artist when I said farewell to Rio with a night photograph, # 3 (see pasted above).

In that photograph, between black and dark gray, the water traces curves of froth on the deserted beach. The undulations of the sea and a diffuse brightness on the horizon can be discerned. Visible on the granulated sand are the signs of almost erased footsteps. Like the other ones I had taken since starting to prepare myself for departure, that was a photograph of my fear.

[July 1, afternoon]

4. The shapes of the problem

Early in the morning I called my mother in Porto Alegre. She gave me news of my two sisters who still kept her company and of the three older ones from her first marriage who had moved to São Paulo with their husbands.

– I'm going to Brasília on business, I told her.

No, I hadn't married yet. No, I wasn't going to get married. Yes, I had settled down. No, no drugs, never again, that was ancient history. No, I had stopped drinking too, not to worry. Yes, it was enough money to cover my expenses and in Brasília I was going to earn more.

– Why don't you stay with one of your brothers? she suggested.

Antonio, who had made a career as an engineer, was the offspring from Mother's first marriage. Despite being only one year older, he talked to me as if he were my father. Mother became a widow, and from her second marriage were born myself, my two sisters, and Gustavo ("Guga"), younger than I am and a university professor in Brasília.

– I'd go crazy if I had to live with Antonio even one day. And there's no room in Guga's apartment, I told Mother, and ended the conversation with words that were both proper and cordial. She had been a Portuguese teacher and was still a language purist. She always corrected both my Portuguese and my deportment. Between the two things, she was content with the easier one—in other words, vocabulary and grammar, carefully packaged in a polite formula.

With the sun already up, I walked along the beach aimlessly, camera over my shoulder, noticing: the choppy sea; the foam swimming around my feet; and the patterns that the water, the wind, and the crowds beginning to arrive from the outskirts of town made on the sand, like in the abstract photo above, in black and white, # 4. I liked to make the photographs indifferent to time and place but the date and the place of that photo became etched in me, like a brand burned into me with a firebrand. The use of the ninety-millimeter lens and the closing of the diaphragm to an aperture of f/16, with an exposure of 1/60 of a second, would permit total depth of field. The morning light strikes a perfect angle on the sand. Each grain of sand appears in perfect clarity, highlighted in a silver impression. I initially called that photograph "The Shapes of the Solution," changing this years later to its current title. I often used titles that revealed what I felt and weren't merely descriptive. Those enigmatic, sharp-textured shapes traced themselves both in the sand and in my mind. Between one distraction and another, an idea became stuck like chewing gum to the bottom of my thought: I'd keep the duplicate keys to Joana's apartment. Then, while I was searching for the perfect angle, combining the maximum amount of information in a slightly asymmetrical composition, I convinced myself that my most basic problem was that I needed Eduardo Kaufman's money to pay the rent if I had to leave Joana's apartment. That's why I'd put aside my pride and principles to be used later during boom times. There on the beach, my most basic problem was taking the shape of an immediate solution that would transport me from Rio to my anti-Rio. At least that's what I thought. I wanted once again to explore Brasília's lunar landscapes, its feminine lines and crimson hues.

July 4

I liked that Carolina brought her friend, the photography apprentice who wants to help me organize the archives. Her name is Laura. Although I could barely make out her shadow, from her voice I discerned her delicate figure. She seems tall and thin. She brought regards from Joana. Laura's parents, ranchers in the Pantanal, have known Joana a long time and she stayed with them more than once.

My goddaughter was in a hurry and left, saying she was late for a reception at the American Embassy. Laura stayed part of the morning.

– Mr. Cadu, I've seen several photographs that you published, she said.

– I forbid you to call me Mister. Don't remind me of my age. We're colleagues.

She wanted to see my archives. I pointed out the location of the boxes with the printed material and of the hard disks with the digital reproductions. To continue my Book of Emotions, *I asked only that Laura open the computer file with the photos of my old photographic diary and help me locate the photograph of some eyes.*

– What woman do these feline eyes belong to? They're beautiful, seductive.

– That was the first photograph I took of a journalist I met when I returned to Brasília.

Let's leave the work for another day, I told her. We talked. She'd always been interested in photography. I concluded from one of her comments that she doesn't have a boyfriend. She lives alone in an apartment rented by her parents.

– Use my darkroom however and whenever you want. You'd be doing me a favor. It really isn't being used . . .

She's from the interior of Mato Grosso. Does she have indigenous features? I felt that her hands were small and her skin very smooth. Her voice is contained without being timid. She liked Marcela and vice versa. Marcela actually whimpered with pleasure at the pats she received.

[July 6, at night]

5. Marcela's eyes

I disembarked in the Pilot Plan carrying luggage filled with photos and cameras. I arrived with all expenses paid and an apartment on loan from Eduardo Kaufman at 104 South. The deal with Eduardo also included the purchase of equipment for my darkroom.

Brasília aroused the rustic fields with green caresses. I rediscovered in it the sensual and audacious wide-ranging poetry that could be read as baroque, then as Arcadian, further along as Concrete, then as marginal poetry and even as pure haikus . . .

I recalled what Joana had once said to me. I spent a Carnaval with her in Rio when I was living with Eva, Paulo Antonio's sister. Eva had remained in Brasília to attend her brother's carnivalesque political rallies. I was in bed with Joana when we heard the shouts in the streets and then the news on television about Paulo Antonio's disappearance. "No fall of the government is worth the memory of our rendezvous, of this bed," Joana said to me. And she was right, despite the tragedies that followed.

Paulo Antonio won in the past, but Eduardo Kaufman wanted to revive the memory of the disappeared former President to pose as the heir to a noble cause, thus increasing Eduardo's chances of being elected to Congress.

– His government matters less than the man and the image of him fixed in the people's memory, Eduardo Kaufman explained in his office in the North Bank Sector. I'm going to finance a TV documentary about Paulo Antonio. These days culture is image. The entire world makes and remakes itself in movies and photographs. And television has the power to bewitch; it gives a different meaning even to trivial conversations.

Later, addressing me:

– Cadu, I want concrete things: photographs.

– What you really want is to revive illusions, I responded.

Everyone looked at each other. Besides Eduardo himself, there was an attorney specializing in raising funds to support culture, a filmmaker, a skinny girl with an expressive face and fine chin, and Eduardo's chief-of-staff in Brasília. Framed by the window, Brasília was its own organic, sculptural promise, the *bossa nova* of architecture. It suspended its monuments in mid-air, full of grace, as its architects intended.

The girl with the expressive face exchanged glances with me. How old could she be? Not more than thirty. Just as I had noticed the generous proportions of her breasts for such a small, lithe body, she surely had appreciated my tall muscular physique. I allowed my eyes to penetrate her white blouse of lightweight wool and her equally white brassiere whose lace trim was discernible. I delighted in those volumes offering themselves uninhibitedly across the table.

I thought: was it possible Eduardo didn't worry that the rumor of the affair between his ex-wife and the former President would be revived along with Paulo Antonio? He should leave that cadaver in peace instead of trying to make a trophy of it.

– Paulo Antonio was downtrodden and resentful.

With this additional provocation, I got another look from the skinny girl, this time a cheerful glance. I prepared my camera. I pretended to be photographing the room, used the zoom and tried to catch the girl who'd smiled at me from a good angle. She fled my viewfinder with the skill of someone avoiding a gun about to go off, and I ended up following the direction of Eduardo Kaufman's finger pointing toward the table.

There was a pamphlet printed with a photo of Eduardo alongside half a dozen Indians, all embracing the trunk of a *samaúma* tree. The photo was accompanied by an explanation of everything that Eduardo Kaufman and the Indians made out of that tree a meter-and-half in diameter and forty meters in height: from the wood they made boats, wood veneer, and cellulose; from the tufts or kapok, buoys and life jackets, mattress and pillow stuffing, in addition to thermal insulation; from the seed, edible oil and oil for lighting as well as soap; and from the water extracted from the roots and trunk, hair tonic and medicine for schistosomiasis.

Not long ago Eduardo had become even wealthier—I was told—with the sale of one of his businesses to a foreign company.

He wasn't just a publicity magnate but the owner of a conglomerate. To pose as a defender of nature, he flooded the market with everything from natural rubber condoms to design objects made with indigenous technology and labor.

– Resentment can produce great works, Cadu, Eduardo answered after some time and several other subjects, as if he had continued pondering my provocation and had only just found the words he was looking for.

– You have to research and document at least one story. It shows how much Paulo Antonio transformed himself into a genuine superhero in the eyes of the people, he said. I don't want to say that it's right or wrong. Reality is reality. History with a capital H embraces popular religiosity and the processes of de-modernization. They're transforming Paulo Antonio into a saint, as they did in the Northeast with Padre Cícero. He materializes in macumba yards. He has worshippers in the Garden of Salvation, starting with the prophetess Iris Quelemém herself. Who is the Paulo Antonio who appears in the macumba yards? What kind of miracles does he perform among his faithful? Marcela, who's a journalist, can research this story.

So the skinny girl's name was Marcela, pretty name. Then he turned to me:

– You should make the photographic history. And there's also Vila Paulo Antonio, one of Brasília's newest satellite cities founded less than ten years ago, with forty thousand inhabitants already. All the work has to have an anthropologist's focus, because the memory left by Paulo Antonio reveals a great deal about our nation's people.

It was already the third time he had referred to the "people." If I could, I would eliminate that word from the language—an abstract and indistinct mass that filled the mouths of demagogues, justifying all kinds of things and provoking heated debate. In the people's name, murders and robberies were being committed and crises created.

– Paulo Antonio will end up exalted by my photographs, in the first place because they don't speak, I said.

– They don't speak? Eduardo asked.

– Better yet, they don't scream.

My brother Guga had once mentioned the advantages of a parliament of the mute.

– Muteness alone would be a great quality in a politician, I added.

Marcela's eyes smiled, if not with approval, then with the recognition that my words made the conversation scintillating. I didn't hesitate. It was the decisive moment. I zoomed in and took photo # 5. Her deep green eyes, slightly startled, like a nervous, wild animal's, were surprised by my flash.

July 11

Once again Laura spent part of the morning here. This time she helped correct the chronology of the photos, which genuinely interested her. She confronted the nudes quite naturally and she liked the flowers most of all. She wanted to know if I had already written about Marcela's eyes and offered to help me with the photo collages throughout my Book of Emotions.

– I promise not to read it. I just want to make your work easier.

I regretted not being able to see the photos she takes.

– I don't take photographs for the sake of taking photographs. My photos are a way of reacting to what bothers me, she said.

Then she shared her opinions about the day's news with me.

I wish I had her enthusiasm. When one is young everything seems new, the future is long, the transformations of the world are frightening with their threats but enchanting with their promises. For old people like me, movement at a distance seems monotonous and repetitive. Laura follows each new case of corruption with an emotion that I can't any longer feel for cyclical things. I believe this is one of the principal symptoms of old age: the sensation of déjà vu that drains dramatic qualities from the present. What does it matter to me that the economic world map has changed in these past two decades? Humanity hasn't changed, and technology hasn't yet managed to dominate nature's fury with its earthquakes and hurricanes. I don't want to say that nothing has improved. No one dies of cancer anymore or even AIDS. But if I can't get enthused for what has gotten better, I also don't feel any revulsion for what has gotten worse. So many new problems have appeared . . . New wars, new diseases . . . Brasília has grown more human and thus more cruel, capable of more terrible crimes. It lost the aura of a futurist city to become a city like all the others.

Laura wants to come here regularly, perhaps twice a week.

– I can't see your photos but I can hear your chords. Next time, don't forget to bring your guitar, I requested.

[July 11]

6. It was March in the window

– I know you're a skeptic, Cadu. But we can't abandon our goals. How to meet them, that's the question, said Eduardo in the apartment at 104, before leaving for the airport.

– And Ana? May I contact her for this project? I asked. Ana was Eduardo's ex-wife who still used the Kaufman name.

– To be honest, it's not a priority. I doubt she could add anything.

– I took many pictures of her.

– Really?

– Beautiful ones. Before the suicide attempt, you must have known.

– Of course.

– And of her marriage to that idiot.

– I lost contact with her. Look, within the month I'll be back for a tribute that Iris and the mediums of the Garden of Salvation are going to hold for Paulo Antonio. I want you to record it.

I called my brothers. Guga invited me to a party the following day. It would be at Paulo Marcos's apartment—I hadn't seen him in ages.

– A coincidence, everyone will be coming over. We're expecting you, Paulo Marcos said on the phone.

Antonio invited me to lunch within the week. His wife was fine, his kids too, both of them so intelligent . . . I couldn't stand listening to all this. The truth was that he endured his wife, tolerated her insults, but one day would yet pick up a gun and kill her, like in a *carioca* tragedy by Nelson Rodrigues. Or perhaps not, he was too much of a coward for that. He was an obedient and good husband, and immune to her assaults. He had a sense of duty and lived for his home and the education of his children, a young girl of thirteen and a boy of eleven.

– Still single? he asked me.

I served myself a twenty-five year old whiskey and, to pass the time, took stock of Eduardo's apartment. I turned on one of his computers and started reading what was there. Eduardo had put locks on some programs and folders which of course heightened my curiosity. At that time I could have been a hacker if I had wanted. I unlocked everything easily. What secrets could I unearth? I discovered that Eduardo had logged onto a site for "the hottest girls on the market, with discreet service for entrepreneurs and politicians," where the photos he had clicked on most often were of a twenty-year old Nisei named Akiko. Akiko enchanted me. I thought about contacting her using an ID with the name Eduardo Kaufman.

By chance I found a list of names that was titled "Operation A." I remembered what I'd read only that morning in the *Folha de S. Paulo*. I reread the article carefully. The Federal Police were investigating an alleged scheme of a slush fund run by the leaders of several political parties, amounting to thirty million reais distributed among almost eighty mayoral candidates in the state of São Paulo. The contributions came from about forty companies, several of them curiously located in the Amazon, clients or suppliers of a well-known state corporation, with headquarters right there in Brasília. The scheme also involved bribes by cashing checks based on fake receipts, and phony consulting contracts and monies from a state-owned corporation paying out money related to percentages designated both as fees and campaign contributions. A police source had leaked the information.

I imagined that a scheme of this kind could form part of Eduardo Kaufman's strategy as he headed for the Central Plateau. The mayors who benefited would soon become his electoral captains in a bid for congress.

I served myself another whiskey. The block was quiet. Not even a horn could be heard. I liked that city. I just couldn't stand being a civil servant like most people there. I couldn't give up my freedom to say and do whatever I wanted whenever I wanted. Working for Eduardo would be temporary. In no time I'd be able to survive on my own. For now Eduardo had allowed me to install a darkroom in his maid's bathroom, but I intended to move it soon to a studio in one of the commercial spaces in the North Wing.

I brought my camera to the window. I sought clarity, black on white, to undo the mystery of the image and recover meaning in the disorder of the things before me. Photo # 6 orders dissimilar things, the natural and the artificial, the living and the dead, and makes them coexist forever naturally. There's a shocking quality to it because it's apparently meaningless and you can't visage why it was created in the first place. The entire afternoon fit into that framed moment. It was March in the camera's eye: the *manacá* blossoms in the foreground occupying the greater portion of my visual field, tingeing their white with pink. Nothing to indicate movement. A dead pigeon lies on the leaf-strewn ground, rigid, with its feet upturned. Four rows of empty chairs slice the photograph on a diagonal. A group of cleaning women, heading toward the left side, take their bosses' dogs for walks. A sensuous sky turns the late afternoon crimson, painting the lawn with a wide swath of light. That could be my first photograph for the enormous flower panel that I intended to compose in honor of Brasília.

7. Quincas Borba and his owner

In Paulo Marcos's apartment I found what I needed: a noisy group that filled me with energy and brought good omens. He lived in the North Wing, at the edge of the Water Hole Park. It wasn't his ministry salary that paid for the leather chairs and sofas, the Persian carpet, the Belgian vase on the sideboard and the paintings by contemporary artists. The good taste and the money belonged to Tânia, his wife.

If Tom Jobim and Vinicius de Moraes had seen Tânia pass by they would have composed their song for her, no matter how great the disadvantage of the North Wing with respect to Ipanema. A Parnassian poet would have compared her to a goddess, but I only say that she was full of grace and that her large black eyes shone with curiosity and intelligence. To complete her pale face, bright and fresh, add a tapered nose more perfect than that of any possible through plastic surgery, a cheerful mouth that made tiny French pouts as she spoke, small ears and short straight hair. I won't even comment on her body to avoid creating the impression that I might have had second, third, or fourth intentions. I can say that it was neither thin like a model's nor full like Marilyn Monroe's. She had perfect measurements for someone like me who likes to feel that there's a layer of soft flesh over the bones.

– As always, you look so . . . , she said when she saw me.

Although the word "so" had been suspended, alone, without any quality or defect to complement it, I was sure that the ellipsis printed on Tânia's contented face was full of good adjectives.

I took a picture of Quincas Borba, the couple's Weimaraner. After making his rounds of the living room, sniffing between the legs of everyone present, he rested his head on Tânia's thighs. My brother Guga, disheveled, uncombed, and unshaven, smoked a joint. I think it was there, on that occasion, that I noticed for the first time a certain look Guga gave Tânia that I wouldn't remember except for what happened long afterward. Future events, like magnifying glasses, enlarge almost imperceptible and apparently unimportant facts.

When he heard the click of my camera, Guga, who liked to quote left and right, repeated with a mysterious air the words he had uttered to me when I decided to be a photographer: "Man's eye serves as a photograph of the invisible."

– Guga came up with the name "Quincas Borba," Tânia told me.

– We're coming to a dead end, Guga mumbled one of his predictable phrases, continuing some conversation that I had missed.

He was paranoid and depressive, which only worsened with drug use. One day he could end up putting a bullet into his brain. His theories were almost always summed up by the observation that life was a long lament and nothing was worth the trouble.

– I wanted to ask your opinion about a project I have. In your field, literature. I'm thinking about writing a book, I told him.

– Are you a bum?

– Not yet, but I'll get there.

– Transsexual?

– What do you think?

– If you're not in the midst of any ethnic, cultural, or racial conflict, your story is of no interest. Unless you fill your story with violence, or write about some disaster.

– I have no literary pretensions. I want to be humbly precise about what I've seen and lived.

– So, what's it about?

– It's a kind of diary, using my photographs; shall we say: a photo diary.

– But still, there has to be a thread to your life to create the plot or the suspense. Or at least your story should be exemplary in some way: it should show that you were able to make something, even if it's a family or a business, do you understand?

I got it. Because of my scatterbrained nature, I had in fact made nothing.

[July 12]

Besides Guga, among the invited guests I met an artist named after Escadinha (known as "Stepladder"), a famous old Rio criminal, and Marcela, the skinny girl with a narrow chin and black eyes I'd seen at Eduardo's meeting.

Some years before, Stepladder had become famous with paintings made of excrement, odorless colored fecal materials, seen by some as beautiful, by others as endowed with superior critical intelligence. Now he was telling me that he was having success with digital photographs on display in the Bank of Brazil Cultural Center. I never called him by his real name. "Stepladder" was more suited to his character. There were diverging theories about why he had earned the nickname. For some, it was because he ingested a lot of cocaine. For others, because he knew how to escape, like the famous drug trafficker who had a helicopter land at a prison. I added a new theory to the others: because he rose rapidly in life.

– I never wanted to be a photographer, he said. I don't understand squat about photography. But by chance the curator of a MASP exhibit simply looooved a work I made with my digital!

The photographs had been published in a book he showed me. They needed more contrast. Their colors were dim with poorly defined grains and blurry zones.

– I don't care about technique, Cadu. I have the photographs printed in São Paulo. Sometimes I ask for adjustments. When they don't turn out, I discard them.

– They're beautiful! Marcela cried.

They weren't. They had an overdose of visual effects, the night colors leaving multi-colored stripes on transvestites, criminals, prostitutes, cadavers . . .

Stepladder had gone to Papuda prison and showed us black-and-white photographs of several inmates he carried in a small portfolio.

– Do you remember the two guys involved in Berta's murder? One of them is this fellow here.

I was shocked. I knew it was my son, whom I'd never even seen; the son of Berenice, Ana Kaufman's current maid. With Berenice it had been a slip of mere minutes.

– I don't care about paternity, Berenice had told me. I'm leaving here, to raise my son alone; I only want money for the trip and to set up my own business.

I gave her what I had and she'd kept her word to never come looking for me again.

In the snapshot Stepladder took, my son isn't comfortable in front of the camera. A sudden movement, by someone who wants to get out of the field of vision, provokes a slight blur in his image. He looks inquisitive and dissatisfied. Part of his face, with an expressiveness accentuated by the bushy eyebrows, is hidden behind the arm that had perhaps been leaning on the wall and now served as a shield, making a movement as if for a fight, a dance, or a macumba step. That hairy muscular arm appearing in the foreground is covered in tattoos. The other arm is dropped, relaxed, with the hand resting on the waistband of his Bermudas, holding a cigarette between his fingers. The open shirt shows his muscular chest and hair. Tall and handsome, he doesn't have the face of a murderer, but rather of a sincere young man who can be trusted.

I had always felt incomplete without a son by my side. If it weren't for the stupidity of believing that the life of a bachelor and no children would help keep the flame of desire burning between me and Joana, I would have convinced her to go through fertility treatments and I would have had not one but several children with her. Despite that, I'd never wanted to search for my only child. Why not do it now? I imagined myself taking that photograph in Escadinha's place. Mine would be different, it would have more respect for the person photographed; it would give my son dignity.

This second time I saw Marcela, my eyes penetrated the voluminous content of her black blouse. Who said that proud breasts stacked on a narrow waist couldn't be attractive? It would be worth descending from those breasts down the exposed midriff, studying the form of the navel until pausing on the angular bones of those hips. I liked to guess whether the triangle between the legs had a little or a lot of hair, if the hairs were hidden down below or if they filled the entire surface of the triangle, if there had been waxing or not, and if this had been done in the form of a vertical rectangle or not. I concluded that Marcela was favored there also, where there was a protrusion out of proportion to a body poorly balanced on toothpick legs. I wasn't a man with singular tastes. If I preferred Joana's splendor and venerated Tânia's classical shapes, I could also appreciate someone who from the back looked modest.

– A coincidence, right? Marcela said. The nose arriving ahead of her body marked her personality with a strong feature. She probably went to bed quite willingly, seriously and with dedication. The wide-open mouth of narrow lips, very narrow, and the absence of a chin reinforced the grace of that body.

– Hey, weren't you in a soap opera? she asked.

Several years before, in a bit part on a soap opera, I'd had my twenty-four hours of fame as a handsome guy. My fame as a lousy actor, achieved at the same time, still lingered among those who hadn't forgotten me.

Why did I feel so great? Perhaps it was because of Tânia's comment, Marcela's question, the good music, the good conversation and of course the good liquor as well. On second thought, the liquor was the deciding reason: four caipirinhas transformed me into a cheerful, good-looking man.

They say that alcohol makes you forget. I can guarantee that it also makes you remember. I remembered Aida. I hadn't seen her in at least a decade. I had always had the greatest admiration for her. She was the one I could have married if she wasn't already married. But I had never even dared to kiss her. Some years before, I got news of her separation. No one at the party knew her. I wondered, had she moved away from Brasília?

I agreed wholeheartedly with Marcela's polite words about each dish and even about the temperature of the beer as a pretext to please her as well as the lady of the house. Our subject in common was Eduardo Kaufman's project for the Garden of Salvation, which provoked Guga's criticism:

– Tell your friend Eduardo not to mix religion and politics. Even before the Inquisition, spirituality provoked intolerance and conflicts. All the world's fanatics, from all religions, think that their God is the best. They establish a direct communication channel with Him to justify every kind of prejudice: against other cultures, other religions, against those who have no religion, against gays . . . They make crusades, jihads, declare war. How much more peaceful the world would be if there were no religions.

– What are you talking about, Guga? You're nuts. There's no intolerance or war there. Iris invented a kind of ecumenical religion; they're open to everything as long as it has a spiritual base, Marcela explained, with her soft voice, gesturing with her hands and raising her eyes heavenward like an altar saint, perhaps because she believed that the spiritual was sublime and superior.

In theory, except for the apocalyptic paranoid vision of things, I could agree with Guga. If it weren't for Marcela's presence I would shut up, because I couldn't put it better than he had. But Marcela was worth my sacrifice and I argued in her defense. I gathered up every bit of intellect and knowledge that I could and gave my opinion that . . .

It doesn't matter and actually I've already forgotten about it. The main thing was that my words were an introduction to an invitation to Marcela. I proposed seeing a light comedy at the Pier. Since the lines were long I skipped the pretense and we fell into apartment 104. Marcela was no Joana, but I was pragmatic. Better a pigeon in the hand.

She wanted to see my photographs. After I showed her the main portfolios and explained my current projects to her, the pigeon escaped from my hands, scampered about the living room and the bedroom, avoiding me, and then flew away. But she left me a promise: she thought it would be fun to be a model for one of my projects.

The next day, the operator informed me that Aida's telephone number was unlisted. I Googled her. Three results: Aida, alongside her son in City Park, was being interviewed on the condition of public bathrooms; Aida signing a petition in support of the homeless; and a notice from the Ministry saying that emails should be sent to her, head of the personnel department. She was separated, and had been for some time. Would she have remarried? Did she have a boyfriend?

I examined the photos from the previous day in the camera. I deleted all of them but one, # 7 (above). Quincas Borba rests his head on Tânia's thighs; she is seated on the floor in a lotus position. The silky coat on his forehead reflects the natural light coming in through the window. There is something human about his expression. Perhaps he doesn't like Guga's longing look at Tânia, a look that doesn't appear in the photograph but that is viscerally associated with it. The crease between the eyes denotes some concern or an air of suffering, and the sidelong glance at the camera is one of mistrust. I set aside that photo and another ten to illustrate the diary that I would start to write and that would go back to my last days in Rio.

July 14

Liberté, égalité, intimité. *Laura and I developed a working relationship that will never, as is proper, go beyond an exchange of friendly, playful words. I clasped her hands. I touched her soft hairless arms and thus reinforced the conviction that she has native blood. Her scent reminds me of Joana. I asked if I could take her picture. I chose the angle. I snapped the camera several times. Of course I couldn't see the result, but each photograph is associated with the smile that I imagined on her face, the words that I heard from her mouth and the smell and delicacy of her hands.*

I asked her to locate a photograph in which a Brasília interquadra sidewalk imitates the Copacabana sidewalks. I can't stop her from reading this or that sentence from my Book of Emotions *when she helps me arrange the photos. But I should redouble the security surrounding this diary, which I must keep in absolute secrecy.*

The significance of the date took me to the Bastille and the French Revolution and from there by meandering paths to my youth, to the only remaining bottle of champagne and to an old song by Serge Gainsbourg.

– I want to raise a toast to our friendship! I said.

– To our friendship! she answered, clinking her glass with mine while we listened to Gainsbourg's song:

> *Aux armes, et caetera . . .*
> *Tremblez, tyrans et vous perfides*
> *L'opprobre de tous les partis*
> *Tremblez! vos projets parricides*
> *Vont enfin recevoir leurs prix!*
> *. . . aux armes, et caetera.*

[July 14]

8. Emotion without meaning

I would have to wait until Monday to call Aida. After taking two swigs of one of the last bottles of whiskey in Eduardo's cabinet, I put the camera over my shoulder and went for a walk through the blocks to the little church of 307. It was Sunday, and more people were attending Mass than the little church could hold. The old, the young, and children gathered outside. I had scruples about taking photographs of the beggar families lined up at a good angle. I preferred the *manacás* and the purple glory trees that could become part of the panel I had planned.

I continued to the Main Axis, full of people walking, running, or riding bicycles. I thought up a new sport: collecting the smiles of beautiful women. I smiled first, and felt good when one of them reciprocated.

I passed a group of marathoners. "Running is fattening," I thought when I saw how many fat people were running. On the Central Axis, hundreds of plastic cups shone in the sun. I placed the camera on the ground. Through the viewfinder it looked like an endless sea with the texture of the waters in *E la nave va*.

Back in the apartment, I connected my laptop and sent Aida an email although I doubted she would check her work email on the weekend.

Sunday afternoon, what could be worse than sitting by myself at the table in the Carpe Diem drinking beer? Then walking aimlessly and spending a long March rainstorm between supermarket shopping and organizing negatives? I realized that during all those years in which I had made a point of living alone, separated from Joana by several floors, I had never really been alone. I sent another email, this time to Joana. If she would have me, I'd run back to Rio.

I made a quick inventory of the bottles in the living room cabinet. I poured half a glass of Danish brandy. I drank it at the window. The block became silent again. I repeated the shot of brandy.

The crickets were now singing that the world was beautiful and living was worthwhile, loving was worthwhile. The day was fading in its slow faint. A third shot and that uniform shadowless light moved me. During those hours, I always fell in love with the landscape. Everything became beautiful: the doorman going by with a broom in his hand, a cute couple crossing the center of the block, children playing ball on the pavement, and, in the distance, beer drinkers in the interquadra bar. All of it should happen at the same time, together with the flying leaves . . . That's why I used the wide angle. So that the emotion that overcame me would be manifest in photograph # 8 (above), all of the space shrunk to fit the camera's field of vision. It's the photograph of an undefinable late-afternoon emotion, with no meaning, composed by the eye of a drunkard who forgets himself at the window.

9. Copacabana in Brasília

I went downstairs and followed the tree-lined path. No one remained in the 304 shopping area. On the left side in the middle of the block, a bar, perhaps an ice-cream parlor, which appeared out of focus in the photograph I'd later take. I drank a coconut water there. At the table in the back, toward the sides of the interior of the block, young people were celebrating some great achievement, or perhaps only their own youth: they got up, hugged each other yelling at the same time and laughed, laughed a lot. The girl at the table in front looked at me. "This isn't going to amount to anything," I thought. I was going to insist with directory assistance that I wanted Aida's phone number. I would check my emails and with luck she and Joana would have received my messages.

The waiter gave me a big smile and said goodbye as if I were an old friend. I crossed the street and slowly examined the imperfections on the ground and the ugliness of the shop windows. Before a bare-breasted mannequin I came to think that Aida would no longer be the girl of old times. Perhaps her wrinkles would have changed her facial expression. But I intuited that the beauty of her body, molded by many years of ballet practice, had not been disfigured by time or by the birth of her son eight years ago. At the end of the interquadra, when I was preparing my camera in front of a Middle Eastern grocery, a stronger image attracted my attention.

In the picture I took (# 9) a blind man is sitting at the edge of the sidewalk made of Portuguese stone mosaic imitating Copacabana's sidewalk patterns. His head is slightly reclined, the right eye shut, while the left, with a milky iris, casts its dead, frozen gaze on the puddle the rain created and in which his body is reflected. In the background, the plaque "104/301." On the ground to his left, one can read the sign: "Help the blind." There's also a package of pens and stickers beside him. He must be exhausted and feeling abandoned at the end of the day. The good man inside me made a point of removing a bill from my wallet and exchanging it for one of those stickers. But the photographer cruelly controlled the scene, told the good man to keep silent and, taking advantage of his invisibility, drew near to find the best angle. The poor man's blindness helped me forget the scruples that in the morning had kept me from taking a picture of the beggars. I was moved and indignant at what I saw, but the strongest sentiment came from taking a picture of that scene and being able to show it to others, to reproduce, preserve, and appropriate it for myself forever. My respect for photography was greater than my compassion for a pitiful wretch. Cold and calculating, I felt like that photographer who between preventing a murder and taking a picture of the murderer prefers the picture. The opportunity that makes the man and the thief, also makes the photographer and his ethics.

[July 15]

10. Photograph of an absence

The memory of Antonieta pushed Aida from my thoughts and excited me as I hadn't been since I'd arrived in Brasília. It was for her and not Aida that I'd felt more lust in that city. More than anyone, she could make me forget Joana. She was a new, younger Joana with an even more attractive body. An athletic, black Joana—a successful basketball player who, as I'd been told, turned down an invitation to pose for *Playboy*. Antonieta exaggerated in her words as well as in her makeup and clothes, but I needed her exaggerations. I'd gone out with her in Rio a year earlier.

– Men are different, they like casual sex, even with strangers, I'd said to her at the bar.

– The same could be true for women, she'd answered.

She'd take a flight to Brasília in a few hours and we'd promised we'd see each other again.

On the phone, back in my apartment, I noticed a tremor in Antonieta's voice. She was newly married or had a steady boyfriend, I didn't get which. Whoever it was, he was traveling and would arrive within a week, that she had told me. And why did she tell me? There was no doubt about it. Brasília wasn't disappointing me. I'd

45

start my long exploration of the south-sector love motels along the highway to Belo Horizonte, in the company of that black body sculpted to perfection.

I could see myself dating Antonieta and having to justify myself to Mother and Antonio. "It's not that I'm prejudiced," she'd say, quickly adding something about the possible complications and practical problems of dating a black woman.

Even if it were just for one night, it wouldn't matter in light of Ana Kaufman's example. I'd had one night with her that had never ended. As a matter of fact, almost all the one-night women had lasted. I counted them. There were many. But Ana had lasted in a special way. Who knows, I might still be able to get back together with her. It didn't matter that she was six years older than I was. She was married to an idiot, that marriage couldn't last.

One detail bothered me: Berenice was now Ana's maid. My son, Berenice's son, was in Brasília. I only knew him from Stepladder's snapshot. I thought about those novels in which the main character, usually the narrator, from one moment to another and as the result of a sudden revelation, a tragic accident, or for some reason or other, decides to find a father, a mother, a father or mother's murderer, a son or daughter, a missing husband or wife, or someone who represents the promise of love . . . I was certainly curious. Sooner or later I would have to meet Bigfoot—that's what they called him. It was as if I'd already an appointment with him and merely didn't know the date. What would he do after leaving prison? Why shouldn't I make my photo essay about Papuda prison? If Stepladder had gotten authorization to photograph the inmates, why couldn't I photograph just one, Bigfoot? But why photograph him, if I wasn't interested in identifying myself, in acknowledging my son and caring for him?

As planned, on Saturday I went to Antonio's for lunch. He lived on North Lake in a completely white single-story house set back from the street. He pretended to be happy with his ordinary life. He'd married a charming temperamental woman who bossed him around and exploded over any little thing.

Like me, Veronica liked movies. With her friends she was amusing. With Antonio, annoying. He suffered in silence and perhaps thought that, for an unattractive dull man, he was extremely lucky to have a woman, any woman, by his side. And not to mention a woman younger than he was! Perhaps they were together because of the children or simply out of inertia.

Taller than Antonio, dark-skinned in a very Brazilian combination, Veronica dressed as if she were half her thirty-eight years. Her frivolous, restless eyes, wrinkled by myopia and slightly crossed, smiled at me. She made a point of showing me the guest room where I would always be welcome, and the children's bedrooms, my niece's neat room with photographs covering the walls, and my nephew's room with clothes and papers strewn on the floor. At the end of the hall, the master bedroom. I noticed long mirrors in the spacious bathroom, one on the door and another inside, in front of which Veronica surely liked to dress seeing herself from head to toe. On the terrace, two straw hammocks were hanging on hooks, ready to be extended. In the backyard surrounded by a hedge were a grill and a small amoeba-shaped pool.

Veronica showed me an article in the *Correio Braziliense* about an exhibit by Stepladder at the Bank of Brazil Cultural Center. A whole page, with photo reproductions and a text titled "A Photographer's Success."

– Since you're a photographer I thought you might be interested, she said.

Stepladder's work didn't have the consistency, the aesthetic quality, or the technical accomplishment of mine. I was confident that time—a patient, unfailing judge—would yet put us in our rightful places.

The feijoada was good and the caipirinha even better. While I was listening to Veronica's complaints, I had four or five.

– I apologize for the feijoada, Cadu. It didn't turn out the way I wanted.

– You exaggerate, Antonio said.

– I accept full responsibility for my mistakes. Now that mess you saw in the living room and the children's bedrooms, Cadu, as well as the overgrown grass, are Antonio's fault. If it were up to me I'd have hired a cleaning woman and a gardener and the problem would be solved. But Antonio is a tightwad . . .

The chatter and the caipirinhas made me sleepy. Veronica put up a hammock on the terrace where I slept until dark. Later she was disappointed that I didn't want to go to the Yacht Club with her the next day.

While still at Antonio's house, I called Antonieta. She didn't want to go out that night. She suggested that I come meet her at Water Hole Park where she walked every day.

– The day after tomorrow very early, at 7:30.

I told Antonio about my plans to date a black woman. His reaction was more measured than I expected.

– It won't work, he declared laconically.

Then he wanted to know if I was going to settle permanently in Brasília. He gave me suggestions for spaces to rent, told me about incentives to open a microbusiness and asked if I paid into any private pension fund.

– Life also means working and building something, he said.

The next day, Sunday, I went to Water Hole Park to rehearse my meeting with Antonieta. The sky clouded over and then the sun lit up the park and the ground. With my camera in hand I took the inside path. From within, the cement shining in the sun, the trees rose like a forest of snakes. It would be a good place to hold Antonieta's hands, to tell her I had never known a prettier woman, that I associated her with Rio, that I had spent months and months thinking about her and the memory of her startled me in the middle of the night, or on a trip to the beach or while watching a movie. Up ahead, a bench. I photographed a mysterious, interior climate by framing only an edge of the bench against a play of light and shadow projected against the gravel background. I would invite her to sit. She might not accept, we'd continue our walk. If the photographs turned out well, they could make up the fourth wall of my exhibition, an entire wall dedicated to Antonieta. I say "the fourth" because the other walls were already full: one with triangles in the style of Volpi; another more intimate, with Joana; a third with the panel of flowers.

Soon the vegetation grew more dense, the path darker, the sun filtered by leaves, no other stroller, "careful crossing this area" the sign said, perhaps because it was a deserted section, not a soul, we could be mugged . . . I'd clasp Antonieta's hands more firmly there, pull her toward me, embrace her whole body, feeling her breasts pressed against me. I'd close my eyes and no kiss could be more real, no lips more sensitive, impassioned flesh one for another, her genitals kissing mine. Looking at the sky, I saw the cloud formations in a sharp picture, layers upon layers. That's what I could photograph to record our imaginary embrace.

I continued walking and went up the small hill, perhaps it would make a better meeting place. Other hills were in view, covered with vegetation. It was as if the stroll had taken place on a rural road that took us to the high rustic bench up ahead. We'd sit on it, I'd stroke Antonieta's thighs and she'd smile at me. One more picture, the tall bench in the foreground and a background of hills tinted with several shades of green.

Later at the lake, the Water Hole lake, toads croaked. On the other side, a small bridge, people running, getting exercise. I didn't know if she was romantic, whether she would appreciate the landscape . . . Antonieta, I only knew the expression of her face and the shape of her body. With the exception of that afternoon in Rio we had never talked for more than five minutes. But if she lingered on the landscape I'd pretend to enjoy the view too. I'd continue to admire her lips and pointed breasts, her ebony complexion, her broad smile revealing perfect teeth.

In the absence of Antonieta's breasts, ebony complexion, and broad smile, I photographed the bridge, the water beneath it, some stones, and the green in the distance, like a Japanese landscape.

That night I received an email from Antonieta. She thought it would be better for me not to come. A tremulous, angry glow from a far-off street lamp twinkled under the palm fronds up ahead. I wouldn't give up, she might change her mind. I called her. She was polite:

– You know what? I don't like to do anything in secret.

– Why in secret? What if I went to the park and we met by accident?

– The thing is, I don't know what you want from me. For me everything is slower. It needs to be built a little at a time. We barely know each other, right?

– Everything starts somewhere.

– It won't work now, Cadu. Someday I'll explain.

I developed the photograph of the Japanese landscape, thinking I'd show Antonieta the charge of desire contained in the image. A photograph of an absence, # 10 (above). Anyone who can't sense Antonieta's absence in that photograph or hear my heartbeats thinks it's just a peaceful postcard landscape.

[July 15, in the afternoon]

11. Quincas's warning of danger

Despite Antonieta's refusal, I went to Water Hole Park the following morning at the appointed time, still hoping to meet her. After two complete loops in which all of the places from the previous day's pictures had lost their charm, I ran into Tânia accompanied by Quincas Borba. A quick glance was enough to notice her nipples were enlarged with pleasure. Or was it just the cold? There were no panty lines under her skin-tight shiny black leggings. I thanked her for the lunch and praised each detail of the apartment, from the Persian carpet to the Belgian vase.

– Don't you want to come with us to Stepladder's exhibition?

– I don't know. I'm so busy these days. I have to get working on the research about Paulo Antonio that Eduardo ordered . . .

Would I be capable of betraying a friend? I thought, walking alongside Tânia. She seemed to like Paulo Marcos, he trusted me . . . I diverted my eyes from Tânia to the landscape and, for a few seconds, my thoughts were carried to a zone of fear and prudence populated by devils pointing their tridents at me. But only for a few seconds. It was her fault, because she was so charming . . . And why did she squeeze my hands while smiling contentedly?

Quincas began to bark, censoring my intentions. Then he went quiet. He seemed to be consenting now. I held her hands firmly, pulled her in my direction, slid my hands around her back and ran them down her curves to confirm that in fact she wasn't wearing panties. Tânia laughed and squirmed away as if I'd tickled her.

– What do you think you're doing?

I didn't think anything, unless confusion of ideas is thought. I wanted and I didn't want. Quincas sensed the danger and barked again. I felt relieved. I took the opportunity to snap his picture. It's photograph # 11. He lifts his head in the direction of the camera and bares his teeth like a wild animal. I decided to leave things at that point, saying goodbye to Tânia with pecks on the cheek. The wise dog had saved me from an embarrassing situation that would have forever complicated my friendship with Paulo Marcos.

[July 15, late at night]

12. Aida

I was finally able to speak to Aida at the Ministry and invited her to lunch at the Brasília Bar. I didn't have much money, but surely Aida would split the bill with me as she had done the only time we had gone out for lunch together many years earlier in a restaurant in North Wing. She was happily married back then, maybe she had wanted me as much as I wanted her, but nothing had ever happened between us beyond an exchange of languid looks and words of affection.

I spent the rest of the morning sorting photographs of Ana and Joana. I sent Joana another email: "Why don't you come visit me? I'm not asking much. Spend a few days here with me, no obligation." Then I went to the bar. It was crowded, people talking loudly, groups of spinsters, beer drinkers, one young woman or other. Could that woman in the back with white hair and wrinkles like the Brasília sidewalks be Aida?

I saw myself as Bertrand Morane, the character in Truffaut's *The Man Who Loved Women*, while I enjoyed my draft beer and the line of women with their backs to me at the buffet who were suspended on platform shoes and high heels. My eyes penetrated their clothes to scrutinize their bodies in the most minute details and the variety of size, shape, fabric, and color of their panties. I had become an expert on the topic. I noticed a tiny pair of white bikinis beneath a pair of slacks that were also white. The curve of the derriere could be Aida's.

Time passes quickly when our minds are distracted, relaxed, and calm. But it almost stops when we impatiently observe the passage of time itself, measuring the minutes with our eyes glued to the clock. Those minutes were the equivalent of hours of waiting.

That's when Aida surprised me, younger and in better shape than I had imagined. She still had a ballerina's carriage. She never stopped smiling while telling me the story of her life in short chapters. She wanted to know if I had a girlfriend, a fiancée, if I was married. I couldn't let Aida think I was a loser who contacted her because Joana had dumped me and left me at a loss, not even able to convince Antonieta to go for a walk with me. No, on the contrary, I needed to display a big game trophy. I spoke of Marcela. No, it wasn't anything serious, I said. Yes, an affair, I wouldn't call it a relationship. I "hooked up" with her, as the kids would say.

Aida was divorced and had an eight-year-old son named Mauricio. She had three sisters, all of them living in Goiânia. I told her about Guga and Antonio, about my friendship with Tânia and Paulo Marcos and finally about Antonieta.

– Antonieta Lobo? she asked.

– Precisely.

– A good friend of mine. We see each other all the time.

While I was talking, Aida let me hold her hands and stroke them.

I suggested we go to a motel.

– You're still the same, hopeless, she said, laughing. No, I'm not up for this. But I want to see you again.

I mixed that austere face with the face from the past, fit that body onto my mental image of it, and in this way Aida continued to be attractive, despite a few extra kilos and a son named Mauricio. In that instant I took photograph # 12 because our eyes crossed with tenderness and intensity. There is sweetness, goodness, and patience in Aida's expression. The natural light from the window directly hits her very pale round face, the face of someone who doesn't get any sun, a few wrinkles visible on her forehead and fair hair falling over her shoulders. The gleam in her eyes is pure and transparent. Between the fingers of her left hand, in the foreground, smoke rises from the cigarette. I noticed her smile smudged by the light nicotine stain between her teeth only after the photograph was developed. It was the smile of someone who admired me as much as I admired her. And mutual admiration was a good beginning for love. Here's proof that photography can store whole conversations and unique moments that are dear to us.

July 17

I try to make myself write every day, but yesterday I had no energy. The dryness of the air has been bothering me. Sleeping little and eating poorly, I caught a cold. I should add that The Book of Emotions has begun to worry me. I imagine this is what authors call writer's block, a block that has settled in because I'll still have to write about Eduardo Kaufman.

Mauricio was here today. Seeing my photographs, he thinks I've had countless girlfriends. He even asked me out of the blue:

– Did you sleep with all these women?

– Only three or four were of any importance in my life, I answered with suspect arithmetic and I almost emended the answer to add two or three. And the most important of them all was your mother.

I didn't show Mauricio my writings. No matter how open-minded he may be or how much he likes me, I don't think he would appreciate what I've written about his mother up to now. I wouldn't need to call so much attention to my inveterate voyeurism that even blindness hasn't cured. Maybe in the rewrite I'll put more clothes on the women in that bar, cover the sheerness with heavier fabrics, darker colors, or less tiny underwear, or even turn my eyes to an antique light fixture, the paintings on the wall, or the hard wooden stools. From my re-union with Aida I didn't forget even the smallest secondary details.

After he left, I continued to reflect on desire and its arithmetic, seen from the perspective of an old man. I'm almost twice as old as Humbert Humbert; on the other hand, Laura is more than twice as old as Lolita, and for that reason, if anything were to happen between us, we wouldn't cause the same scandal as Nabokov's characters. And for me there would be the advantage of feeling younger, since as I imagine the best medical manuals say, love with a younger woman is like a tonic. With Laura by my side I would live at least another twenty years, and the longer we live the more the difference in our ages that had at first seemed far apart narrows. If today Laura is only a little more than a third my age, in twenty years she'll be half my age.

I discovered a very concrete meaning for the expression "either eight or eighty." It's clear that Laura is no longer eight nor has Joana reached eighty. If we add eight and eighty, we can take the average and I should be happy to stay in the past with Aida and her forty-four years of age.

July 18
I just walked around the block twice with Marcela. My cold feels a little better and I try to resume my routine.

[July 18]

13. Ana in her splendor
Eduardo called me around that time. He didn't tell me what he was doing in Rio but I guessed that he was with Joana.

– I need the selection of photos of Paulo Antonio, he demanded.

– It's not ready. These days I've been browsing through photos of Ana and other girlfriends (I mentioned Ana on purpose). But I promise to go to the Paulo Antonio Memorial. And I'll do research in my personal archive.

He insisted that he wanted a sample a week from then, when he would arrive for the tribute to Paulo Antonio at the Garden of Salvation.

I rearranged the bottles in the living room cabinet to hide the missing ones. The empty spots on the shelves had grown in exact proportion to my binges.

A week from then, I woke to Eduardo Kaufman invading my bedroom. Of course the apartment belonged to him; even so he was still an intruder, arriving unannounced. I reluctantly accepted his invitation for lunch at Piantella. After waving to several regulars he told me that the bald man in the back was Congressman So-and-so, a scoundrel and his political archenemy.

– Corrupt? I asked.

– That I don't know. But he must be. Who wouldn't be if he were sure to go unpunished? These guys have special judicial privileges. Only the Supreme Court can judge them.

This guy back here was the Minister of Justice; that one, Senator What's-his-name; the dark woman whispering in his ear was a social columnist; the man standing smoking a cigar was a well-known political commentator . . . With my camera over my shoulder and threadbare clothing, I stood in contrast to the others and in particular to Eduardo, wearing his Armani suit, briefcase at his feet.

Through the large horizontal stained glass window above, a yellow light projected onto equally yellow walls. An air-conditioned chill moved down my back. We both ordered beer and chateaubriand.

– And the selection, is it ready?

– No. Organizing Ana and Joana's photographs took longer than I expected.

– You're going to use Ana's photographs in your exhibit?

– I haven't decided yet what to do with them. Do you want to buy them?

– Either you do the research I asked for or I'll have to hire another photographer, got it? You can stay in the apartment as long as you want, just so you prove to me each week that the project is progressing. Marcela has already produced some of the texts. She said she tried to show them to you . . .

Marcela, who had agreed to model for my triangle panels project, thought I wasn't very professional after I tried to kiss her when she was standing naked in front of me. I explained to her the meaning of that series of photographs for which I didn't hire models because, although the photos showed only an anonymous piece of the female body, it was essential to have a story behind each one of them.

– I don't want to be part of your collection of women, she said, irritated.

In short, I'd grown bored with Marcela and that's why I hadn't returned her phone calls.

– Would you sell Ana's photographs with the negatives?

Rationality was prudent, patient, calm, and gentle, like accepting the invitation to work on the project with Eduardo Kaufman. Madness was intense, impassioned, and violent. It spoke louder, like the hatred I felt for him. I wanted the courage to make mince-meat out of him, to send him into orbit. Or at least to ask him about Joana. Three glasses of beer hadn't been enough to do it. Out of that anger, a touch of reality finally distilled an exorbitant price for Ana's photos.

– Deal, Eduardo said, without batting an eye at the price. But I'm afraid our project is coasting. Have you at least set up the darkroom? I don't want to get to the point of making you show me the receipts to prove that you actually spent the money on equipment . . .

Before delivering Ana's photographs to Eduardo, I'd make copies. There were no nudes. They were chaste photographs, in black and white, the sensuality and melancholy obvious in the eyes and the facial expressions. As one can see in # 13, reproduced above, Ana's beauty was unconventional, imposing itself firmly in her slanted, almost oriental eyes, full lips, black hair, and a nose that I wouldn't say was large, not to give the impression of disproportion, when everything about her seemed to be made to express her intelligence and personality perfectly. She's reclining on the sofa at her house in the position of an Ingres odalisque, the curves of her tall, brown body highlighted by the black dress.

[July 18, night]

14. Harmony, by a hair

Aida wanted to see a movie about gangs in the hills of Rio, the crime and drug trafficking underworld, that was showing at the Tennis Academy. I quoted Guga:

– This is demagoguery glorifying violence and crime. They substitute plots with a disaster or an extremely violent scene.

– It's reality, Aida argued. Things are like this and someone has to show them.

– Yes. Reality is reality, I said, with a dripping irony she didn't notice, repeating the phrase Eduardo Kaufman had spoken at the meeting a month earlier, and I added:

– And dreams aren't real? The comfort of the rich? And isn't my own life real, spending every day doing nothing, not having a single disaster, not being robbed, not confronting any bandits or coming into contact with criminality?

– But there's no narrative in that. It wouldn't make a movie.

– For me, more real than the violence is living with the fear of violence without ever facing danger. The movies don't have to convince me that the newspaper articles are right. I don't even need to read the papers.

– If the violence doesn't seem real to you . . .

– Maybe it's just a question of probability. The probable doesn't happen to me, and the improbable winds up happening. I can sleep out in the open at the bus terminal or leave the door of my apartment open and I won't be robbed. I can plant myself in front of an ATM rubbing my credit card in the thief's nose and I won't be the victim of a kidnapping.

– Don't be so sure, my dear. What's the most improbable thing that ever happened to you?

– You appearing in my life.

– I was about to tell you something: you're a photographer, my dear; photography is the only art that requires a concrete, real object before it. More than cinema. The essence of photography is to represent reality, you know that.

– An instantaneous, fleeting, and sometimes deceptive reality.

– The fact is that you can doubt a story or a painting but no one doubts a photograph. If it shows something it's because that thing was there, it was real at least for that moment. And what photo do you think would be more realistic, one you take of the Ministries' Esplanade, the Three Powers Plaza or a session of the National Congress, or another, showing Vila Paulo Antonio? If it's a question of probability, there is a greater probability of finding misery and violence in that Vila than here in the Pilot Plan. There's where you'll feel the people's drama. Behind each photograph, a tragedy. Do that, Cadu, go take photographs some day in Vila Paulo Antonio instead of wasting time with your nudes.

– That's exactly what I'll need to do for Eduardo Kaufman.

– Or at least do realistic work. I don't know if you saw that exhibit by a famous artist, a painter who does photography now . . . What's his name? He ran the risk of confronting criminals, then he took a series of photographs at Papuda . . .

I preferred to ignore the reference to Stepladder. I wasn't the only one to whom the probable didn't happen and the improbable ultimately did. Stepladder's success was improbable. It should be more probable that quality would be recognized and banality relegated to oblivion. Well, my work wasn't lacking in quality, and Stepladder's overflowed with banality. Some blind curator had appreciated his mediocre work and given him notoriety. What did it matter to me that Stepladder ran risks taking his photos if the result was a low-quality commercial product, packaged for the market like a bar of soap? Where were the critics who didn't recognize his sham or my genius?

I thought about confessing to Aida that the reality Stepladder portrayed was closer to me than to him because my son was imprisoned at Papuda; showing her how poorly portrayed Bigfoot had been by Stepladder, who hadn't even interested him in being photographed. What a joke, a photograph in which the subject was trying to leave the scene! How much better I'd do if I took his picture!

– You haven't even been to the satellite cities, Cadu.

– I confess that I went as far as Taguatinga but I didn't cross the border of Ceilândia.

– That's unforgivable, Cadu. Let's go to Samambaia together, to Vila Paulo Antonio and the other cities.

Fellini's *La Strada*, a mixture of cruelty and poetry, was showing. That was my salvation. We went to the Academy in Aida's car, a blue Golf with several years of use. The story of Gelsomina sold to Zampano by her dirt poor mother touched Aida, and that allowed me to hug her as if I were protecting her from a monster.

Since it was raining when we left, we sat at one of the tables with a view of the lake to have coffee and ran into Veronica and Antonio. She was in high-heeled sandals, wearing a short white skirt and a blouse with ruffled straps. I liked the silver braided earrings that moved with her restless head. They had seen the violent film Aida had initially suggested we see.

– They're the new romantics, I said. They'll soon be able to show the most horrendous massacre and dissect the cadavers in the public square.

– That's been done, Veronica said.

– There will always be more, cutting flesh into small pieces with the victim still alive, being abused and suffering the most terrible pain before dying. With the public present, of course, just like in the Roman arena.

– That's been done too, you're behind the times, Veronica said with laughing eyes.

We compared the poverty and the realism in the two films and, to reach an agreement faster, I didn't argue with Antonio's conclusion:

– Reality is reality.

Afterward Aida wanted to stop by her house to pick up Mauricio. Every weekend he went out with his father and by then he should be back.

– How was today with your father? Aida asked Mauricio when we arrived.

– I don't want to go there any more.

– He demands Mauricio's presence because he won that right in court, but he pays no attention to the boy. He's always busy. That's the main reason for our separation. He's self-centered; he thinks only of himself, his work, even on the weekends. Mauricio is losing patience, right honey?

– He's a pain, Mauricio answered.

– But he's still your father, I told him, thinking about my son who certainly would have an even worse opinion of me: a father who had run off, who had taken no responsibility and had never contacted him.

Mauricio made a face. I would have to work twice as hard now to win back his affection. We stopped by 104 to pick up the photography bag I always liked to carry over my shoulder, and then the three of us went to a nearby restaurant at the end of an inter-quadra at the start of South Wing, a spacious, open place. It was impossible not to become involved with the neighboring table, to hear the yelled conversations and the whistles to the waiters. We got in the buffet line—paunchy men in Bermudas, women in tight clothes, short, tall, thin, fat, obese, big round rumps, tiny flat bottoms, groups of women, men, older couples, young couples . . . We sat at a table for four outside.

– We look like a perfect couple with a beautiful son, I said.

Mauricio didn't appreciate the compliment. He was still serious and didn't want to talk to me. A group of Koreans came over to try to sell us junk, watches, mechanical stuffed animals, alarm clocks, radios, and pens. I spent some of my paltry change on a toy for him: a bright yellow fluffy chick that ran around when you pressed a button.

Aida made me a sudden invitation. She wanted me to go with her to church on Sunday. She proved to be a Catholic with sympathies for the evangelicals and who believed in miracles.

– The closest I've come to religion was taking photographs of Iris in the Garden of Salvation, I replied.

Aida showed genuine interest in the Garden and was surprised that I knew the famous prophetess personally.

– She had disappeared for a few years. This only heightened the faith of her followers. She's very old now, I explained.

The efficiency of the waiters was measured by the speed with which they brought another draft beer as soon as the glass was empty. Mine emptied five or six times, and Mauricio began to play with the cork coasters printed in red with the beer logo that came with every glass.

I prepared my camera, on the lookout for a spontaneous gesture from Aida or Mauricio. I'd like to appear in the photograph but I couldn't, because at the same time I wanted to be behind the camera, to be the eye catching the flicker of happiness making itself visible in that misshapen environment. I tried to find an angle that would show the trees in the background. The *manacá* blossoms were beginning to change color from pink to purple, alongside the violet hues stamped on the purple glory trees. The uniform light of the already-set sun lit Aida's and Mauricio's faces to perfection. I bent down to snap the picture. Mauricio sat up straight posing. No, better to leave the shot for later. I waited for a moment of distraction and bent down again. That time Aida was turning to the side, calling the waiter, and the light already wasn't the same, it having gotten dark. A lost photo, an almost-photo, that missed capturing the harmony of the afternoon by a hair and that, by mistake, I kept in my files. It's # 14, which can be seen above.

[July 20, after midnight]

15. Mauricio at eight years of age

I taught Mauricio a trick: with a fast slap on the edge of the cork coasters, I flipped them and caught them in the air. Mauricio learned the game quickly and was soon doing it better than I could. I asked him about school, teachers, friends, about Brasília . . . I asked him about his block too, what he liked best and what he was going to be when he grew up. I let him pose and collected several happy expressions. One of them can be seen in photograph # 15. Tall for his age, Mauricio raises both arms as if stretching, his right hand holding the left. The dark background of the photo contrasts with the yellow of his T-shirt where the number ten is visible. His gaze is confident and naughty. He's totally comfortable in front of the camera.

– You're going to be my friend, right? I asked.

– I already am.

July 21, pre-dawn

I keep this simple phrase more present than ever because Mauricio today is my best friend and even my confidant. Days ago I showed him the pictures of Laura. He praised them and, from everything he said, I concluded that I had been right on target: she's attractive, although of a beauty not grasped at first sight. I drew a picture of Laura in my head. Blindness has the advantage of composing beauty with more elements than mere physical appearance—whose outlines are traced by touch, which feels the object more closely than sight.

– I don't know if it's true, but physically she reminds me of Joana; and in spirit she has something of your mother, I told him.

I immediately regretted giving the impression that I was interested in a twenty-five-year old. He wouldn't understand if I explained that I like to hear her voice and imagine her figure. Just stopping by, saying good morning, for me that's a lot. She fills my days with life, and that can't be dismissed by someone who already smells the stench of death. I mentioned her intelligence and sensitivity. He doesn't know her yet but seemed to agree with me. I asked him to open a file of very old photographs of Joana, to compare them to the ones of Laura and confirm for me if the two women look alike.

– Not at all. They're different types of beauty. To start with, one is blonde and the other dark.

– *The blonde hair is dyed, I explained.*

Laura has been coming here every week but she'd never given me a hug as affectionate as today's. Maybe she was happy to see me almost recovered. I felt her body, her breasts touching my torso. Could it be that after a certain age you lose the right to feel the physical presence of a beautiful woman? If the Creator exists, he had a sadistic impulse when he inoculated an old man with desire for a young girl.

And me, what do I arouse in Laura? I have to be realistic. Reality is reality: she has the same affection for me that she has for a grandfather. I'm lucky to be blind so I don't have to see my wrinkled face every day in the mirror. But women are surprising. There are some who don't dwell on physical details . . . In my grandparents' generation it wasn't absurd for a thirty-five-year-old man to marry a girl of thirteen. If we multiply both numbers by two and, keeping things in proportion, maybe it wouldn't be totally absurd if Laura and I . . . I need to put these thoughts out of my mind. I'll be satisfied to capture her perfume with my nose and the delicacy of her voice with my ears. Who am I to have the right to love her? But dream of her embraces, why not?

We barely worked. I felt an unexpected pleasure in showing her some photographs of clothes on a bed, photographs of Joana's absent body, which she had the courtesy not to ask questions about. I didn't identify Joana. She thought the photographs were "fabulous!" That was the word she used, with an exclamation and everything else. She saw fetishes in them, praised the framing, the angles, and what she considers my style: the geometric, almost abstract placement of the photographed objects. I set aside the best of those photographs for my Book of Emotions.

As promised, Laura brought her guitar. To say that she doesn't sing well would be a euphemism. She sings off-key. Off-key with the soft voice of someone who has a soul of crystal. Or could it be cotton?

July 22
Today I dreamed a strange dream about Joana in which she said, "Don't die before I arrive," but she had already arrived, she was standing in front of me dressed entirely in white. I awoke wanting to add a few pages to my Book of Emotions.

[July 22]
16. How simple matter seeks its form

I would put off the work Eduardo had commissioned for another few days. Let him wait. My priority would be to show my current production. On a wall, I would install three gigantic panels of geometric photos, recalling multicolored Volpis, a forest of pubic hair in several shapes: triangular, rectangular, diamond-shaped, elliptical, Gothic, baroque, with short mustaches or luxuriant hairs. My search for the absolute. I had snapped the camera thousands of times like someone who takes possession of the photographed object. I collected those shapes like someone who files and catalogs experiences; like someone who wants to keep a piece of the world for himself. To simplify things, I would call all those shapes, even the rectangles and ellipses, simply triangles.

I poured myself a shot from the last bottle of whiskey and spread some slides on the table. I began studying the triangles one at a time through the viewer. Some were happy, others sad.

Some of them had the luxuriance of a tropical forest, others looked like savannas or deserts. One of them consisted of very pale skin, the part the bikini had protected from the sun, profiled against a suntanned body. From the center of the triangle curly hairs also descended in a triangular shape. The hairs darkened the closer they came to the vertical slash at the lower vertex. On the edges of the black triangle in another photograph the hairs seemed like delicate little pencil strokes and they allowed a glimpse of dark skin. The closer they came to the center of the triangle the more dense they became, like the vegetation growing along the banks of a river. In another slide, sparse hairs were crowned by a tattoo above the top portion of the triangle. Below, an acute angle was sliced in the middle, and little round lips appeared on either side of the vertex. In another photograph, lace climbed like vines in the shape of an isosceles triangle.

I liked geometry and didn't limit myself to those shy, reserved triangles. In contrast, more than half the photos belonged to an uninhibited, wide-open series in which the legs spread for my camera, as in the painting *The Origin of the World* by Gustave Courbet. It was a series of inverted trapezoids or vertical rectangles, within which were set ellipses of closed or open labia, flaccid or engorged, opaque or shiny, framed by fair or black hairs, in small or large quantities. One of the photographs recalled a dry leaf, the central line well drawn, from which lateral fluff emerged. It looked liked Joana's, but wasn't; Joana had never exposed herself this way for my camera; the nudes I'd taken of her were stolen images, while she was sleeping or bathing, and they wouldn't work for those panels. One more photograph, long bearded labia funneling downwards, a protuberance in between them, like an atrophied tongue or penis. That other image didn't show labia exactly, just little wrinkled mounds that rose from the central valley. I chose a minimalist photograph of transparent fluff sliced by a clear straight black slash.

With the women photographed from the rear, the triangles were inverted and cut through the middle, from top to bottom. One of them looked like a plump shiny fruit with two rounded segments. In another photograph, an ellipse sliced down the middle in perfect symmetry was bordered by an external ellipse. Still another showed the internal ellipse frightened and agape, revealing crimson flesh inside. I recalled each woman and I hadn't forgotten their names.

I asked Guga's opinion of my choices. Smoking a joint, he said:

– They're photos of unfulfilled desires. Of suffering.

– How do you know?

– I don't mean to say in the physical sense. I mean, as an idea of the search for happiness.

– I'm not looking for happiness.

– You don't understand what I mean. We desire what we don't have. Unfulfilled desire causes suffering, and every fulfilled desire is replaced by another. But there's no escape, my friend. Life fluctuates between suffering and boredom. You've chosen suffering. If you manage to free yourself from your desires, it will be boredom. Unless you can learn to see the world like a Buddhist monk, in a disinterested way.

– Enough philosophy, Guga. What do you think of the photos?

– If you want me to be honest, they're monothematic and, for that very reason, soporifically boring.

– Every photograph is unique. No image is ever the same as any other and it's for one very simple reason: because no moment in life is ever repeated. Do you agree?

– In the case of your series here, that dimension of photography is lost.

– Guga, look at the huge variety of shapes! The photographs aren't homogeneous, dear fellow. No way! And then, there's interest in what's behind each one. Also in their textures, outlines and volumes, not to mention the subtle dialog among the triangles.

– Do any of them belong to your girlfriend? I realized he was referring to Aida.

– She hates these kinds of photographs.

– You told me she's very religious.

– That's not why. She prefers me to show something she defines as "realistic," a photo-essay about the poor or criminals.

– Good idea, but it depends on how you do it. Photo-realism has no reason to hide the photographer's presence. I like photos in which you feel the collaboration between the photographer and the subject, understand? They can reveal more of the subjects' personality than if the photographer made himself invisible in order to capture spontaneous natural images. Not only should the photographer show himself to the subject. He should also use the camera as a brush, to focus and unfocus planes, blur scenes and show the trail of movement. This way, he can create an expressiveness that reveals the characters' interior state of being. A good example is Stepladder's work. It has merit. He took photographs of several convicts at Papuda, I don't know if you've seen them.

– Look here, if I took pictures of convicts, you can be sure that I'd do a better job than Stepladder. Even he acknowledges knowing nothing about photography. And one thing is certain: I would never imitate him. Through my photographs, I want to take possession of something just for myself. Like planting a flag in virgin territory. I'm not interested in entering territory that's already occupied.

Unless I met Bigfoot, and he let himself be photographed, I thought. But even in that case, unlike Stepladder, I wouldn't just take photographs of a convict. My photos would mirror a concealed emotion; they'd have a distinctive quality because they'd contain my secret. Why not visit him? Why not photograph him?

– I wouldn't be able to live with someone who's deluded by saints and miracles, Guga said, referring to Aida.

– Well, for me it doesn't much matter if a woman I love believes in an evangelical Christ or a Catholic one, in a macumba priest or even in Santa Claus.

I believed in the physical world, in what I could touch, in other words, in Aida's body and not in her beliefs. Thinking about this after Guga left and about our plans to visit the Garden of Salvation, I poured myself a brimming glass of whiskey. The sunlight traversing the windowpane passed through my glass. That's how photo # 16, which I set aside for my photo diary, came about. At that moment, contemplating the rays that stretched across the mahogany table from the glass and sensing how simple matter seeks its form, I had the idea to create a chromatic movement in each one of the panels of triangles, from top to bottom and left to right, including dense dark pubic hairs, dense fair hairs, sparse dark ones and sparse fair ones. I'd finish at the bottom right with the absence of hairs, showing the genitals in clear vertical strokes. Someone seeing the panels from a distance would say they were compositions of flowers or fruits, in shades of yellow, black, and red. Despite showing body parts that are usually hidden beneath layers of clothing, each of the photographs—and also the assemblage—would take on something subtle and mysterious, as if I'd manipulated their colors and added a filmy veil over their surfaces, as if coarse desire had been given a careful polish.

[July 23, almost midnight]

17. April flowers

There would be an intimate wall in my exhibition, dedicated to a single person, only hinted at by the detail of a piece of underwear, a lock of hair or a fragment of a profile. They'd be photographs of Joana or about her, a tribute that I'd secretly made to her over many years. Photographs that Joana didn't know about. And what if she came to my exhibition? How would she react when she recognized a detail of her body or her clothes?

All the women of the world combined weren't worth one Joana. I'd send her a postcard. I'd simply say: "You are unique." If she allowed me to smell her scent, caress her skin, spoon in bed as we had until recently, she didn't even have to say she loved me.

I called her. To my surprise, this time she answered. A good sign. I begged her to let us try one more time to live together and I left her with the impression that I'd be grateful for a few crumbs of her good will.

– Just one week together, that's all I ask. Come to Brasília or let me come to Rio.

– What's the point?

– Don't you miss me even a tiny bit?

She didn't answer.

– I miss you a lot, I said.

– You just want a woman, any woman, beside you.

– Joana, come to Brasília, even if it's only for a weekend (I reduced my request still more).

– I'll think about your case.

Hearing those words, I felt like the victor of a great battle.

If I had many photographs of Joana and too many triangles, flowers were in short supply. With them, I would add still a third wall—and even a fourth—to my exhibition, provided I managed to collect a sufficient number of them. I found them right there in the block. I took photographs of the April flowers, the silk cotton trees, with their pink edges and tufted white centers. Those photographs made my day. I chose the one that seemed most vibrant, joyful and delicate. It's the one seen above.

[July 24]

18. Two or three incomprehensible things

I finally found a pretext for calling Ana Kaufman: to invite her to accompany me to the tribute to Paulo Antonio organized by the prophetess Iris Quelemém.

– I found out from Joana that you were in Brasília, she said.

Cold and laconic, she declined my invitation. But soon afterward I got a phone call from Carlos, her husband. I was surprised by how well he treated me. So he didn't know what had transpired between

Ana and me? I wanted to see Ana, not him. Now I was obligated to go to the couple's home in South Lake for lunch on Saturday.

– It's in your honor, to welcome you, Carlos told me.

I would surely see Berenice and maybe I'd have news of my son. On the appointed day, as soon as I arrived, Ana said:

– We have a surprise for you.

She didn't want to tell me what it was. I should wait. I instantly thought of Bigfoot. Could Berenice have mentioned something to Ana? Would they bring him to meet me?

There were no noticeable marks from the burns Ana had suffered less than a year before. No scars, nothing. Only to someone who knew, some marks camouflaged by clothes and makeup. She looked quite rejuvenated, perhaps from the plastic surgery.

Filling the trays of the CD player, Carlos read the titles of the songs through his Coke-bottle glasses and made comments on the interpretations under the attentive gaze of Josafá, Ana's cat.

– Beautiful poster, I said, pointing at the wall.

– It's a reproduction of a Barnett Newman from 1965 when he was in the São Paulo Bienal, she explained.

In one corner of the dining room a painting by Stepladder flirted with the grotesque.

– Do you know the artist, I mean personally? I asked Ana.

– Of course. He's the only one in Brasília who's any good.

– I see you hold me in high esteem.

– I'm not talking about photographers, but painters. And you're not from Brasília.

I almost protested that there was nothing of mine on her walls, not even a snapshot. That was the difference between her appreciation for my work and Stepladder's.

The doorbell rang.

– The surprise has arrived, Ana said.

Joana appeared at the door in a dress that I'd never seen, more elegant than ever, as if she'd come for a ball. She'd come to spend just a few days in Brasília, she told me. I didn't dare ask if it was to see me, but I trusted that my phone call had contributed to her decision.

At first she treated me distantly. But after two whiskeys she seemed to relax. I even held her hands as if we were two lovebirds.

– How's your project with Eduardo going? she asked.

I told her about the ceremony in the Garden of Salvation.

– I invited Ana, but she doesn't want to go.

– I have a certain level of curiosity. I'll go with you, Joana said. Will Eduardo really be there?

– He's coming just for this.

I moved closer to the flowers in the garden and started snapping the camera looking for a less common angle. My gaze attracted everyone's attention. They surrounded me and looked where I looked as if they were seeing the blooms for the first time. Josafá also came closer as if it wanted to know what was attracting our attention and started wandering around the garden.

– I'm thinking of starting a flower business. I already have a large number of seedlings. If I can cultivate roses, I'm sure I can make money with flowers more suited to this climate. And I'm not talking about dried flowers, Carlos said.

– I don't know a thing about plants, I said, but if you need photographs of flowers . . . They tell me I should be inspired by Stepladder and take photographs of reality. But don't you think flowers are part of reality?

– According to a Buddhist principle, reality is a void, the ultimate nature of things. Reality doesn't exist, at least not permanent reality, Carlos said.

He spoke with a professorial air. Now retired, after spending years closed up in the Congressional Library, he didn't miss a chance to show off his bookish knowledge. He was still a bookworm. He lived through his reading, through other people's stories. He contented himself with Ana, flowers, and books.

– Maybe I can use one of your photographs in a publicity campaign, Joana said.

– No, I'm not interested. They're very special. I'm thinking about mounting an exhibit, I answered categorically, without knowing whether she was referring to some commercial for her store or to a project for her publicity agency.

Two works occupied positions of prominence in the living room. One was signed by Ana Mariani and had been shown in one of the São Paulo biennials. There were photographs of houses and more houses in the interior of the Northeast, all in the same style, with variations in color and angle of light. Another was by Jac Leirner and showed business cards collected from all over the world in a series.

– I want to show a work similar to these, I said. Panels of triangles.

– Triangles? Ana asked.

– Oh, really? You never told me about this, Joana said.

– Love triangles? Ana teased.

– No, it's more a physical thing.

– But are they urban photographs? Nature photos? Of people? Joana asked.

– People.

– I don't authorize you to use any photographs of me, Joana said, as if she could guess my project.

– Your photographs don't fit into my plan.

– I also don't want to see any of those photographs exhibited, do you hear me? You know, Joana, he took some photographs of me last year. They're great!

Finally Berenice appeared. She greeted me politely. It wasn't rare at a party, particularly in Brasília, for me to count the women with whom I'd had an affair. My name wasn't Don Juan and my reckoning hadn't reached *mile e tre*, but at that moment it was enough to have gotten to three to provide for a unique situation: it included all of the women present.

I took a big swig of whiskey and summoned the courage to follow Berenice into the kitchen. I wanted to know about our son. Financial help I couldn't provide. But maybe it was time to meet him.

My courage didn't arrive in time. Halfway down the hall I detoured into the bathroom while Berenice continued into the house.

Later, when the whiskey had caused the predictable effects in my head and legs, I proceeded unsteadily into the utility area to talk to her.

– I didn't ask you about your son. (I couldn't bring myself to say "our son.")

– Don't worry. You don't owe me a thing, or him.

– I heard he's in jail.

– A great injustice.

– I'm going to visit him.

– No, don't even think about it. He doesn't know anything about you.

Later I asked Ana:

– Do you know Berenice's son?

– He's a complicated guy. He was involved in Berta's murder, I don't know if you knew. He should soon get out of jail. He identified everyone involved and he'll benefit from a plea bargain. But he was straight with my nephew Termite. In fact the two of them didn't participate in any of it. They were unlucky. They were with a bad crowd and were present when everything happened, that's all.

Berta had been brutally murdered the year before. Decades earlier, when we were young, she'd been part of our group of "the Useless" together with Joana, Ana, me, and some other friends.

– Did he live with Berenice?

– No. He has a house in Vila Paulo Antonio.

That was the housing project both Eduardo Kaufman and Aida had mentioned and that according to Marcela had been built on lots with false deeds. For the first time it was making sense to equip myself with an anthropologist's eye in order to take photos of that new satellite city as part of the project Eduardo Kaufman had devised.

When we left, Joana gave me a ride in her rental car. Her look was free of all animosity and had something maternal about it.

– There's plenty of room in Eduardo's apartment. Why don't you . . .

– No, I'm well-situated in a hotel. I prefer it this way. I didn't come here to stay with you, she answered, guessing at my plan, but, perhaps noticing my disappointment, she added:

– We can have a drink in the hotel bar.

The bar was at the back of an enormous hall where lonely women circulated on the lookout for politicians or civil servants who came to Brasília without their families, businessmen who travelled here to lobby, and other men passing through to attend meetings. It was a weekend, many of them had returned to their hometowns and there was an obvious imbalance between supply and demand.

The marble floor, as well as the glass and metal tables shone, reflecting the blue and yellow lights flanking the mirror on the wall behind the bar.

– Do you have an exhibition space? Joana asked.

– I'm looking for one.

– I want to see those photographs.

– I'll show you. I really want your opinion.

We had a whiskey. I was carefully testing her interest in me as if I had to seduce her for the first time.

– You can come up with me if you promise you'll behave, she said, after she drained her glass.

– I swear on the Bible. I opened my right hand over her whiskey glass.

– I don't want to hear about sex, I want to make that very clear. It's nothing against you.

– But don't you miss . . .

– I need caresses . . . That's what I miss.

I misinterpreted her, because when she got to the room she refused my kisses, my massages, and my proposal for a bath together. We had some soup and then watched television holding hands, with her sitting close.

– If you want, you can spend the night. Just to sleep, she emphasized.

She didn't desire me like before, that was obvious, but she allowed herself to be seen as she got ready for a bath. Seeing Joana undress was like taking a full shot of vitality that went all the way up my spine to my head. As if vitamins of youth and joy flowed between my legs. I wouldn't trade Joana for any other woman as long as I could see her undress at that moment, a moment which I appreciated in each and every detail, gazing at her arched body, at her panties sliding down her long thighs, at the fullness of her derrière. I knew every millimeter of that body, from the shape of her hands to the black mole among her pubic hairs. It had been a long time since I'd asked her to show me her "beauty mark," which was what I had nicknamed that black mole.

Then we slept together. Just slept, and I was happy.

[July 25]
Preparing for Eduardo Kaufman's arrival, I spent the next few days sorting photographs of Paulo Antonio hugging the elderly, sitting alongside children, running in the park in shorts and a T-shirt or holding rallies.

It was hard to judge the value of many of the photographs without knowing who was standing alongside Paulo Antonio. In some cases the unknown individuals added a quality to the photo: beautiful, half-dressed women at Carnaval; those pretty grape festival queens; figures, uniformed, bedecked or identified by messages on caps and T-shirts, like priests, generals, and union or Landless Movement leaders. In some photographs, one could deduce from the protocol that Paulo Antonio was posing with other heads of state. In several, it didn't matter who was at his side; they were meaningful only because of Paulo Antonio's reaction: for his look of surprise, his laughter, grimaces, tears or his pensive, dreamy gaze. Over here is an enormous Brazilian flag inflaming nationalist instincts and offering a Paulo Antonio embraced with the nation. Over there a crucifix brought his good intentions into the foreground and gave the impression that God was beside the President. I felt all-powerful: it was no exaggeration to believe that my photography could help create the past, history itself. With the gamut of photographs at hand, I could invent Paulo Antonio after my own fashion.

At the Paulo Antonio Fernandes Memorial, I found the photograph taken on a Carnaval viewing stand minutes before his disappearance and also a copy of one of my photographs, the first one from my file number one. It's the famous photograph of Paulo Antonio's inauguration on which the novel *Ideas for Where to Spend the End of the World* is based and in which his sister Eva, with whom I lived, and the Prophetess Iris Quelemém, from the Garden of Salvation, among others, appear. The copy, which I still keep in an electronic version, has one advantage over the original. It has incorporated the patina of time. Its edges are torn, there's a slightly yellow stain in the background where a Ceschiatti sculpture and the Burle Marx gardens are visible. It has acquired an air of nobility, sealing its historical relevance.

In May, Brasília's perspectives were still spattered with the pink of the silk floss trees. A flock of parakeets flew away from one of them when I approached. They announced something mysterious, so that an unbeliever like me could take fuller advantage of his trip to the Garden of Salvation. Joana would come with me.

I would take photographs of the gullibility stamped on serious faces and the illusion that not only does a heaven exist but also a magic formula for getting there.

In the outdoor area of a bar I drank some awful cachaça, despite Joana's protests. People looked at her elegance with deference as if she were a queen, a princess, a first lady, a soap opera actress, or, at the very least, the wife of some politician. There was an air of a political rally, people gathered at the entrance to the main temple, awaiting Eduardo and Iris Quelemém.

Finally, a path cleared so that the two of them could enter. Seated in her wheelchair, Iris blessed Eduardo who was standing next to her and to the other priests, facing the multitudes. Smiling, he shook everyone's hands.

He looked surprised when he saw Joana. He hugged her, gave her kisses on the cheeks and made a point of placing her next to him for a photograph that I refused to take.

– I understand. You came here to see Eduardo.

– It's crazy you'd think that of me, Cadu. And why would I have to come all this way to see Eduardo?

For him the photographs were more valuable than the tribute itself. They proved the existence of the event in which he, Eduardo, was the highlight. That's why he wanted to have his picture taken at every moment. He was always focused on my camera and was transformed in front of it.

He went up on the viewing stand and gave his speech. According to the theory I'd been developing, politicians should be measured not by their ideology, but by decibels. The most convincing speeches were the most inflammatory, like Eduardo Kaufman's was that afternoon. Iris was also taken to the viewing stand and placed beside him.

– This woman is really a saint, said a priestess in a fluttering dress, with several transparent capes in blue and pink.

– If it weren't for the money, I wouldn't take these pictures, I commented to Joana.

My role was to photograph the tribute and, as part of it, the session in which the spirit of Paulo Antonio himself would descend. And it did. It grunted and muttered with a drunkard's voice:

– I bless thee. Thou shalt build an evangelical temple here. Give it my name.

– He of all people, who was a good orator and knew how to arouse an audience. Here's the proof that the supernatural doesn't need the brain, which rots with the body here on earth, eaten by worms.

Joana laughed at my comment.

– The company of the Catholic saints up there in heaven must have been a real bore. That's why, after dying, Paulo Antonio became an evangelical, I added, whispering in her ear.

I noticed Eduardo Kaufman's annoyed look in our direction.

Iris was invited to speak. She looked at the sky with her visionary eyes. She raised her folded hands toward something invisible, not simply the building's ridge beam or the mermaid suspended from the ceiling or the Yemanjá drawn on one of the walls, or even one of the macumba saints lined up at the top of the temple. No one understood what she was saying, but everyone agreed with her emphases and with the determination deduced from her strong gesturing. People were carried away by her anger about what had been done and what hadn't been done and by her courage to confront everything and everyone. No one could remember a single word she'd said, but they'd never forget her enthusiasm and indignation. Photograph # 18 is one of many that I took of her gestures or expressions. Three fingers in her right hand were upraised, while her wrinkled face lit up when enunciating two or three incomprehensible things. Three fingers of Joana's left hand appeared on the left side of the photograph conversing with Iris's. They ended up in the photo by accident but harmonized the scene like a perfect translation of what was unintelligible. Joana wanted to whisper something in my ear at the exact moment I'd snapped the shutter, and her wind-blown hair brushed my face. I wanted to hug her, to kiss her, but I didn't feel sure yet of her reaction.

[July 26]

19. Traces of desire

    – Adam means man, humanity; it comes from *Adamah*, from the Hebrew earth; from *adom*, red, and *dam*, blood. The beginning of the world and of humanity is here, in this red soil—so taught a medium with short, hairy arms and plump, disproportionately large hands for that body. He wore a brown T-shirt accentuating a pronounced belly, over which hung a gold chain with a crucifix, a *figa* talisman and a Star of David.

    – Chance doesn't exist, he continued. Everything is foreseen and everything will happen. It's a matter of time; what isn't revealed today will be revealed later. The book already exists in its entirety in eternity and the word that hasn't been spoken yet will be spoken one day. Evil can turn into good and good into evil.

– It doesn't matter whether worms eat this imbecile today or a century from now. It doesn't matter whether I document this tribute or not, I whispered again in Joana's ear.

– May I take a picture? I asked the medium aloud, moving in closer. Joana accompanied me.

He posed for me, happy. Then, to gather more natural expressions, I pretended to be interested in his philosophy, which led him to invite me to his theology classes every Sunday in the Garden of Salvation itself. I promised I'd be his student.

– You're no good, Joana told me, when we moved away.

– From this medium's words one could conclude that the truth has no more merit than a lie. If we don't live today, we'll live some day. It doesn't matter whether I do good or evil. But, no, not everything is indifferent, I said to Joana. For example, whether Eduardo pays me or not isn't indifferent.

I went to find him and demanded my money. In exchange, he reminded me that I owed him work. He counted up the photographs I had produced per day and arrived, as a result of his division, at a mere fraction of a photo. Joana watched us from a distance.

– Why should I have to worry about the number of photographs per day? I answered. Your life, not mine, is ruled by time.

The next day, Eduardo said:

– You managed to exhaust my patience. I no longer need your services. It's not just that you haven't done enough work . . .

– You didn't like the photos?

– I feel you're not interested in the work. Stay in the apartment a few more days, if you have to, while you decide what to do.

Making a living only from my photography wouldn't be easy, but I was filled with joy. I felt like a free man, and I would use my freedom to dedicate myself to personal projects.

I poured the rest of the whiskey from the last bottle in the cabinet into a glass, and rummaging again through one of Eduardo's computers I discovered above all that I was free to denounce him. An Excel file contained the same list of that "Operation A," only this time the names were associated with amounts of money. I didn't know if it was contraband, favors, tax evasion, influence peddling, drug trafficking, or illegal campaign financing . . . But there was something there. I heard rumors about spurious investments by pension funds, overbilling state corporations for publicity . . . Laws were disgraced. I wanted to contribute to the moral enobling of the nation, which was in my personal interest as well. After all, Eduardo had robbed the country and stolen my wife. I was free, and my freedom would be expensive for Eduardo Kaufman. I remembered the kapok tree and the picture of him alongside the Indians. Natural and indigenous products must be a front for some illegal dealings. It occurred to me that the crime passed through the Central Plateau, but the letter "A" meant "Amazonia." I would send an anonymous letter to the Revenue Service with the lists from "Operation Amazonia" and I made plans to return to Rio with Joana.

I reviewed the photographs I'd taken of Eduardo in the Garden of Salvation. There was a close-up of his face: a gaping mouth showing all his teeth, furrowed brow, arched eyebrows and tousled hair. My revenge was just beginning. I would enlarge this photograph that without my realizing it would someday become a landmark in my work. It gave me the idea of composing the *histrionic series*, which, as I intend to make clear later, would earn me some notoriety.

   – I've become homeless. May I move to your hotel? I proposed to Joana, without telling her that Eduardo was letting me stay in the apartment a few more days.

   – I'm about to leave.

   – Will you take me with you?

With the excuse of saying goodbye, I went to see her, bringing a thicker wedding ring in my pocket than the one she had refused in Rio. I stayed, until she wanted to sleep, without being thrown out of her room. I was full of hope. It could be a new beginning. She didn't even protest when I undressed and lay down beside her.

When Joana and I were two strangers she placed no limits on her debauchery. She refused nothing. That's why I can say that until today I've never done anything more daring in bed with any other woman. But suddenly, maybe a year earlier, from one moment to another, she didn't like this, and even less that, she didn't want it this way but that way. I had been living with her long enough for misunderstandings, suspicions, and complaints to begin. Intimacy had put an end to the enchantment of our relationship.

Even so, during many months something had remained: I could feel her body. Even if she didn't want to make love to me, she let me hold her from behind in bed before falling asleep, and I stayed there with my body glued to hers. She didn't protest when my erection pressed against her ass. I only regretted that, after all those months and before our break-up in Rio, she had become so creative in the variations on a recurring theme: it was late or she was tired or she wanted to sleep or she had just woken up or her arm hurt or not today, Cadu, another day . . . Sometimes the lie came followed by a yawn, at other times when I insisted, feigning deafness, by a "no." A "no" that also had its variations: it could be terse, yelled, cried, whiny, a "please, no," a "fuck, no!" or a "no" made explicit by a shove. When summer arrived, the same lie came packaged in a truth: it was too hot, she said, her thighs exposed by the short see-through nightgown. "Don't press," or else "don't touch me, I can't sleep like this."

Now, lying on her side in the Brasília hotel room, I would bear her refusal and even her scorn in exchange for that lost privilege, a remnant of love. With my look and my touch I would erase what was going through her mind. At the moment our bodies touched, everything could begin anew. Our brief separation would surely have intensified how much she missed me. Who knows, we might even be able to recover the first sensations of our naked, embracing bodies.

She was succinct:

– Don't start.

I contented myself with the hope of gluing my body to hers the next day.

But the next day I made the mistake of showing, at her request, the portfolio for my exhibition. I started with the flowers, a still unfinished series. Then I showed her the triangles, which irritated her so much that I decided to tell her about the tribute I would make to her on a special wall. It was pretty tame stuff: the hem of a dress, her feet, a fragment of her face . . .

– Look, Cadu, I tried. It's no good. You've gone beyond all boundaries.

– Is it because of the photos?

– No, it's not because of the photos.

– Look what I had brought for you. I thought of . . . I showed her the wedding band.

– You don't understand anything at all. There's no point in arguing.

Then she said:

– Eduardo told me . . . How did you blow this opportunity? You're an idiot! Totally irresponsible!

It had been a mistake to believe that without the worries of the joint management of a home and the raising of children we would have only the good parts of a marriage. Without the bad parts that handcuff two people together, Joana had felt free. She didn't need me for anything, I was disposable.

I took one final step before Joana's departure. What are the ethics of photography? What image would it be permissible to steal, to appropriate? Taking advantage of her bath time, I removed from the closets intimate items that had touched her body: two tiny pairs of panties, silk stockings, a pearl necklace, diamond earrings, a floor-length dress, and a pair of shoes. I took pictures of them on the bed from different angles—see photograph # 19 (above). I slowly smelled and kissed her panties like a priest does with a stole.

– Here's Joana's body, I said solemnly, aloud.

I wouldn't use those photographs in my exhibition. Unlike so many others, I didn't want to remove them from their private, intimate sphere for public consumption. I wanted to keep them for myself, to appropriate what they represented, Joana's inert body permanently offered to me. I wrapped the new wedding band she had refused with my profound sadness and a black lace panty that I tucked into my pocket.

I still have the photographs of triangles printed on paper. On the back of each one is a pseudonym. I wanted to throw Aida off the track in case she wanted to know to whom they belonged. Over time I stopped associating them with their real names. My memory isn't what it used to be. I've forgotten most of those names by now without ever having forgotten the body of each woman, including the texture and exact shape of their triangles.

I would have made even larger panels with the women I couldn't have. I remember them as much or more than the ones who wanted me. I didn't dare approach several of them out of scruples, respect, shyness, fear of the ridiculous or because I considered them inaccessible. Other women didn't find me attractive . . . or rich enough. Some of them, direct and sincere, told me: "I'm not interested." Still others became silent, smiled with scorn or changed the subject before my passionate declarations, to later transform me into a source of mockery with their friends. The compassionate ones gave me a consoling kiss. There were also some who engulfed me with praise as an introduction to a "sorry, I don't love you." I could fill a whole book with these cases. Not a book, a treatise in several volumes, but it won't be written because I need memories that make me happy and give me the will to live. For this reason, and also in order to impress Laura, I prefer to go to the triangles.

Today, I prepared for Laura's arrival. I took a long shower, put on shaving lotion, trimmed my finger and toenails, shaved and reshaved, trimmed the hairs in my ears and nose, donned my best clothes, and waited anxiously almost the entire morning.

Laura didn't hug me, but she saw the triangles and that excited me. I imagined the impossible: that one day she'd want to pose nude for my camera. It would be an unusual experience because I would be taking photographs of what I can't see and she'd be showing herself to a blind man. To compensate for my blindness, the photographs would be made with the aid of touch. Laura's soul wouldn't be made of crystal or cotton as I wrote days ago, but of an ember that ignites, and I'd be there to feel the heat of that fire. I immediately put that insane idea out of my mind. After all, I don't believe in a soul.

But it wasn't inappropriate to show Laura how I'd enjoyed myself with so many triangles and how I'd been the object of desire for attractive women like Joana. This way my worth would increase in her eyes. Women rarely confess the truth: they like competition and men in demand, not the ones who dedicate themselves exclusively to them. I know this from Joana. I measured her love on the scale of jealousy, the small vain passion of those who demand exclusivity. And when I decided to abandon everything else and every other woman to dedicate myself only to her, she traded me for a scumbag who attracted girlfriends with his money and power. Returning to my market value in Laura's eyes, I know that I shouldn't be interested in someone who could be my granddaughter. But reality is reality, as the scumbag in question said. I won't deny it. I'm interested in a reality whose name is Laura.

She was amused by my research on triangles and wanted to know which one was Marcela's. After so many years, I saw no problem in describing it so that she could find it. I remembered well the rectan-

gle composed of pubic hairs nicely trimmed on four sides, bordered below by two swollen naked lips, in whose center appeared the tip of a tongue like the clapper of a bell.

– Wow! she exclaimed laughing.

No one these days would pay a cent for my notions of geometry or for all that triangular vegetation. By a quirk of fate only the many photographs I took of Paulo Antonio Fernandes and Eduardo Kaufman are still of any value. In fact, Carolina brought me a potential buyer who also expressed interest in my photographs of the Plateau flowers. She's the director of a research center at a foreign university who's putting together a photographic archive about Brasília. She says she'll pay me good money, digitize all the photographs, and even make me two prints of each one.

July 31, night, almost August 1
Mauricio hasn't been here in days. I had the idea of inviting him and also my goddaughter to have a few beers one afternoon. I need to create the maximum number of opportunities for the two of them to meet. It's so obvious they were made for each other . . . I have to convince them of this obvious fact.

[August 1]
20. Politicians and oysters

I could survive without Eduardo Kaufman, although I'd had to adapt to lower-quality drinks and, worse, my newly-acquired freedom was spent taking photographs of weddings and baptisms.

I looked for work through friends. When I called Guga, he'd already heard from Tânia that Eduardo had fired me.

– That fellow is an asshole, he said.

– The worst thing is that he's so dishonest.

I described to him the documents I'd sent to the Revenue Service with a very convincing cover letter.

– An anonymous letter? Then nothing will come of it. You need to send this to the press.

I told Aida that I'd have to return to Rio if I didn't find clients.

– And in Rio? Do you have anything to live on?

– No. But there are more opportunities. I know more people. I didn't tell her that I hadn't given up on Joana or that the biggest advantage to returning would be proximity to her.

Paulo Marcos seemed cold on the phone.

– And Tânia?

– I don't know.

I don't know? I didn't dare ask him.

I called Marcela. She seemed happy to hear from me. Through her recommendations I got a phone call from the owner of a famous restaurant who hired me to document his birthday party. I invited her to go with me.

– I'm in love. And when I fall in love I'm one hundred percent faithful. You know, Cadu, I think I've found the man of my dreams: good, faithful, affectionate, and intelligent. She only neglected to add: "as opposed to you."

– I'm inviting you solely and exclusively to accompany me.

I couldn't convince her and went alone. If it were possible, at the party I would have photographed the women's perfume, the conversations about politics, and the nouveau riche garishness. The few attractive women—not a single one as beautiful as Joana—

either avoided me or smiled at my camera, not at me. Could it be the arrival of old age? Or did they foresee my failure?

They preferred, of course, to see themselves in the company of easy success. There among the women was Stepladder. He greeted me as if to say: "Look where I am and where you are. Me, I'm here as a guest, and you're struggling to survive. Me, I have it easy, and you're killing yourself with work. Me, I'm a great artist and you, merely a birthday-party photographer."

Even though I was working, I had several glasses of champagne, which compromised not just my balance and my stomach but also the quality of the photographs. Nevertheless, there were things to be photographed: politicians of various persuasions and oysters of various sizes. Oysters and more oysters fell from ice waterfalls over giant basins—the ones in the photograph above, # 20. Fresh oysters, brought the same day from Ceará.

The fat man with the mustache in the center of the photograph is the owner of the restaurant. The others are politicians. The interest in that photograph is in the presence, to the right of the birthday celebrant, of Eduardo Kaufman's enemy, the congressman he pointed out to me at Piantella. When I saw him—short, protruding belly, a few blond and solitary hairs emerging atop the shiny baldness, and a pale, frank, and decided ugliness—I quickly devised my plan: I would give him the ammunition to annihilate Eduardo Kaufman. I couldn't continue to wait indefinitely for the Revenue Service to take steps. Not long before, I learned that he was part of a Parliamentary Commission of Inquiry. The documents found in one of Eduardo Kaufman's computers needed to reach his hands as quickly as possible, and they would be the tip of the iceberg.

He met with me several days later. He thanked me for contacting him, he was interested in the papers I showed him and agreed they indicated at least some irregularity. However, it would be necessary to have evidence, evidence, evidence. What else did I know about those lists? How had I obtained them?

[August 1, night]

21. Boss arbitrating dispute over computers

From birthday to birthday and baptism to baptism, I came to the conclusion that my freedom hadn't increased when I stopped working for Eduardo. I felt like the poor do, I was free to complain and go hungry. Just as the athlete of a certain extreme sport throws himself down hundreds of feet knowing he's attached to a cable that doesn't allow him to crash to the ground, or like the trapeze artist who sees a safety net beneath him, I saw the advantage of a job that would guarantee the basics for my survival and let me dedicate myself in my spare time to my not at all lucrative projects. Ignoring Guga's opinion, I considered showing my triangle panels to the curators of the space in the foyer of the National Theater, the Bank of Brazil Cultural Center, and the Gallery of the National Savings Bank.

It was May of 2001, and the reliable pillar of my radical sport became the Ministry where Aida worked. She introduced me to a female friend, a department manager. I was interviewed and got a job. My first job. Aida was offering me the deciding reason to postpone my return to Rio. I'd be a service contractor, with the right to a room in the basement along sprawling long corridors, something like a small city with its winding streets and Middle Eastern bazaar, and where it was possible to find vendors of meat, sweets, and fresh fruit. I shared a room with several employees wearing green uniforms. My principal task was to photograph the Minister shaking visitors' hands, always sitting on the same group of sofas, with the same wall in the background, where a photo of the President, a map, and a flag were visible. I also took pictures of department directors on similar sofas or speaking in the auditorium to a bored audience.

On the first day, I overheard a conversation between the director of our department and her department managers, and thus attended my first class on the management of cunning and pride that occupies the greater part of a manager's time.

– I only ask for opinions from those with something to say, she affirmed.

No one would ask for mine, I thought, while I busied myself with the paperclips in the little box in front of me. I picked up one and bent it back and forth until it broke. I picked up another, stretched it like a wire, then broke it in half. I opened a third and left it standing balanced on the table like a sculpture on a pyramid base. With a fourth, I made a square. With another, I made a ring that I wrapped around my finger. And from these wires I extracted one idea after another and prepared my camera for the right moment, because a good photographer moves like a jaguar confronting its victim, and the final leap results from a combination of opportunity, patience, and agility.

– You have to find a creative way to deny this news item, the director ordered her communications aide.

She had the smile of someone trying to be nice. Her aide returned that smile with another from someone whose job was to please. Although I had never worked in a government office, I already had a basic familiarity with public administration, where the competition wasn't based on work results but on recognition by management, and, for management, accomplishments were less important than a news item.

Suddenly, two uninhibited department managers started to fight in front of the director over three new computers. The art of photography is to capture the moment in which the characters' expressions and their body language reveal something of their personalities, just like in the theater. Something dramatic, sensual, dumb . . . Or ridiculous. I didn't invent a thing in that photograph—# 21 (above)—which recalls a Vermeer painting. I didn't seek angles that would distort the expression of any of those characters. I was simply there, as ready as photographers should be to practice their precise art. And precision exists in the light illuminating each face, throwing a tenuous glow over the table, highlighting the patterns of the carpet and dividing the space into fields of dark and light. It also exists in the expression of each of the subjects and in their nervous exchange of glances.

22. Raise day

There was general dissatisfaction. Complaints about the irrelevance of the work, the disinterest of the Minister in the employees, ill-timed reforms, new policies, the manager's personality . . . Then in one afternoon the policies and reforms recovered their prestige, the Minister and the manager their affection. The miracle, printed in the good humor of photo # 22 (above), was achieved by the salary increase. The person at the center, arms raised and eyes satisfied, shouts the news, which irradiates joy in anyone moving along the first floor corridor. It's the photograph of a joy comparable to a carnivalesque explosion. The good humor the photograph was able to preserve lasted only until everyone became used to the few extra reais and began to consider them too little to cover their increased cost of living.

[August 2]

23. Violeta

My expression must have been like a shiny, giddy, elastic ball bouncing from floor to ceiling and ricocheting from one wall to another until it gave off sparks as it hit another shiny metal. One afternoon when I laid eyes on Violeta's languid face, there were so many sparks they left me dizzy. From my meager office experience I had already figured out a golden rule: not getting involved with work colleagues, even if we were in different areas, with me in the basement and Violeta on the first floor. It would be annoying to have to pay attention to them and alleviate their sorrows when it was just supposed to be casual sex. They would become too friendly or too unfriendly. The photograph I took of Violeta— # 23—was at her request. She looked at me with her brown eyes, a mix of disdain and seduction, as if a model on a runway, a face half lit by the window's natural light and a glow on her serene red lips. Using my professional mask, I kept the necessary distance between photographer and subject. I would strictly obey my golden rule.

August 4, pre-dawn
I think Laura is growing tired of me. When she came by yesterday
she went right to the darkroom. The coldness in her low, prudent

voice bothered me. She hadn't worn perfume. She barely greeted me and didn't offer to help me continue selecting photos. Her steps were loud, as if she was pounding the floor in anger. Does she think I'm an old teacher trying to seduce her?

I had to ask her to please put two or three photos I had written about in order. That was all she did, hurriedly, without even mentioning the old Beatles and Caetano Veloso songs I put on for her to hear.

Later Carlos phoned. I wasn't expecting his call. How kind.

– How are you, my friend? What have you been doing? he asked.

– I'm writing my memoir from the perspective of a man twenty years younger.

– Then I need to send you one of Ana's favorite short stories; I don't know if you know it. It's by Borges, the title is "The Other."

I immediately remembered a literary discussion between Guga and Ana many, many years ago.

– I don't think I've ever read it.

– I'll send you two versions: one for you to listen to on the computer and a printed one that someone can read to you.

I was unfair to Carlos in the first pages of this diary. If I said that I outlived all the friends from my generation who still live in Brasília, it's only because he's older than I am and I never really considered him a friend. Still, he's the only one left from my former circle of friends. I like to get his calls and his kind-hearted attention. Noticing a catch in my throat, maybe left over from my last cold, he gave me some serious advice, and was sincerely worried about me.

After we said goodbye, my seventy years came knocking on the door, took control of me, brought me to this armchair, relaxed my muscles and my thoughts, and left me alone with my past. During *the remainder of the day I listened to the computer voice speaking what I've written up until now. The choice of a man's or a woman's voice, old or young, high-pitched or low, makes a difference. I put on a young, male voice, but there's no way to avoid a monotone on the computer that makes me frightened and tormented. The solution was to listen to Mozart's Symphony No. 41, the Jupiter, with Marcela at my feet.*

[August 7]

24. Of a woman's scorn in a cat's eyes

It was a cold clear day, the start of winter. Aida didn't want to go with me to Ana Kaufman's house. She didn't know her but already hated her.

I rode with Tânia to keep her company because Paulo Marcos had gone to São Paulo. She wore the sincere affection of deep friendship on a face that was almost bare of make-up, and was dressed with the casual elegance I've always associated with *cariocas*.

I brought Ana new copies of the photos I'd taken of her fewer than two years earlier, the same ones I'd sold to Eduardo. I'd already given her some others at that time, but after cropping and careful darkroom work these were clearly better . . .

Ana and her cat Josafá had an airy way of looking, of moving their heads and settling into the armchair. Josafá, with his lustrous yellow coat, silently exhibited his interior life and white paws. He scorned me as much as Ana did. She barely looked at the photographs I'd brought. She seemed more interested in my brother Guga, with whom she started a literary conversation. The two loved Borges and traded views about his short stories.

– My favorite book is *The Book of Sand*, Ana said.

– Is that the one with the short story about the sect of the thirty? According to the rationale of many members of the sect, someone who eyes a woman, coveting her, has already committed adultery in his heart . . . Just look, Tânia! Guga was staring at her like the leading man in a *novela*. Then all men commit adultery. And since desire is no less culpable than the act, as the text says, "the just can give themselves up without risk to the most outrageous lust."

Tânia returned his look and laughed, although with a laugh that to me seemed pro forma, from someone who laughs to be polite.

It pained me inside, an unacknowledged frustration, that Ana was being condescending to me, looking down at me with a superior air. And I who thought that a woman who had been mine, who had given herself in such a complete way, could be reconquered . . . I took a photograph of Josafá and recorded Ana's scorn for me in his facial expression. That's what can be seen in photo # 24 (above).

25. Feels like Sunday afternoon

On the other hand, Carlos had good whiskey. He served me a triple.

– Weren't you going to bring your girlfriend? Ana asked me. I'd told her I'd be coming with Aida.

– She didn't want to come.

– Is it serious this time, Cadu?

– Not just this time . . .

– You know what I mean. Do you think you'll get married someday?

I almost answered that I wasn't married by choice; I was convinced that a man's desire was roving and raced from one woman to another.

– You act like my brother Antonio. I've been married several times.

– Sorry, I'm not criticizing. But you never took your relationships seriously. You didn't even take your marriage to Joana seriously.

– Tell me what you've been doing, Tânia said.

– Nothing. I'm dedicated to leisure. After trying too many different things and failing at all of them, I've concluded that nothing is worth the trouble. I was echoing one of Guga's lines whose meaning I was beginning to understand.

It wasn't a manner of speaking. I'd grown tired of looking for meaning in meaningless things. I didn't expect anything from life or love, I didn't even hope to overcome life's emptiness or escape the void. Even so, this situation didn't leave me melancholic like Guga or resigned, but rather relieved and combative. Without the anguish of someone fearing defeat, I made an effort to reach my goal, which was mainly to vanquish my worst enemy, the one who had robbed the country and stolen my wife—Eduardo Kaufman.

– Cadu's going to found Brazilian nihilism, Ana ironized.

– It was Emperor Septimius Severus who said: "I was everything: nothing is worth the trouble; *Omnia fui, et nihil expedit*," Carlos said, displaying the Latin of a former seminarian.

– You're lazy, Cadu. With your talent, you should get to work, set up your darkroom, Ana said.

– It is set up and dedicated to weddings, baptisms, and birthdays. No one has hired me for funerals yet.

– If you want, I can suggest your name to the artistic director of the National Theater, a good friend of mine. She must need a photographer for the tribute to Paulo Antonio that she's organizing.

– Paulo Antonio was worshipped for the wrong reasons. For nationalism. For megalomania, Carlos said.

The blood went to Tânia's head. She turned crimson when she got worked up. She passionately defended Paulo Antonio. She had unwavering opinions when it came to politics.

If I had known how to say it intelligently, I would have said that politics didn't interest me. I let Guga keep the discussion alive:

– In this country, anyone who isn't a populist or an authoritarian is both things at the same time.

– Don't exaggerate. Liberal traditions do exist, Ana said.

– Liberalism can't survive in the face of so much poverty, Guga replied.

– If Paulo Antonio weren't black he wouldn't have been as popular, Carlos responded.

– To the contrary, the old racial discrimination created distrust and rejection in many people, Tânia said.

– One thing is certain: ideological differences today count for little. The urgent problems are hunger, disease, and ignorance. And there aren't that many ways . . . Ana tried to change the focus of the discussion.

– I agree that the main difference among politicians isn't ideological. They can be classified by decibels. The ones who yell the loudest are the most convincing, I said, thinking of Eduardo Kaufman's inflamed discourse in the Garden of Salvation, expounding in public for the first time the theory that I'd been developing.

– That's why, Guga, what matters most today is being a good manager, Carlos continued with Ana's rationale. And dividing lines exist between the corrupt and the uncorrupt; between the demagogues and the problem solvers; those who see only their private interests and those who are concerned with the common good. And you're right, Cadu, there's also a difference between someone who wants to make the case based on blows and bellows and someone who knows how to lay out his reasons calmly.

– We need to improve the institutions so we don't need to depend on the quality of the individuals, Guga explained.

– Eduardo isn't behind this tribute, is he? Because if he is, he'll veto my participation, I said to Ana, referring to her proposal for the National Theater.

– No. He'll probably be there as a guest. No more than that.

– He's a typical example of a demagogue, Carlos said.

– Demagoguery, amplified by the media, is the essence of politics. Appearing to do is more efficient than doing. Whereas doing can provoke undesired reactions, any second-rate actor like Eduardo Kaufman exerts a seductive power in front of the cameras, Guga said.

What bothered me was that he was a thief. What had the Revenue Service done with my letter and the documents I'd sent?

– I really wanted to have an exhibition of my work, I explained to Ana.

– I'll remind my friend about your Paulo Antonio photographs.

– Now I want to show another kind of work.

– You have beautiful photographs. You should show them, Tânia agreed.

– The problem is that no one's interested . . .

– We've a friend who opened a gallery. I'll tell you right now, the location is strange. But that aside, the space is wonderful. What kind of work would you show? Tânia asked.

I vaguely mentioned the panels of triangles as abstractions based on the geometric arrangement of body details, something that recalled, as I had told Ana earlier, those two paintings in the living room—the one of photographs of a series of houses and the one that showed labels and business cards. I also wanted to dedicate a wall to Brasília, through plants and flowers, juxtaposing the rainy season with the dry season.

Walking around the garden looking for a better angle for a photograph, I met Termite, Ana's nephew. I had seen him on several occasions, the last time about two years earlier.

– If you need white dust, the good stuff, come to me. I have some strong weed too.

When the sunlight lost its sharpness and the shadows stretched along the ground, I recorded the Sunday afternoon atmosphere that enveloped us all in the panoramic photo above (# 25). In the foreground, a carpet of crimson blossoms. To the right, wooden columns through which the pool can be seen. In the background, to the left, the interlaced arches of the JK Bridge, like a flower. In the center, the printed proof that Tânia and Guga's eyes are meeting. They talk animatedly on the terrace shaded by fronds from the carnaúba palm, while the Paranoá Lake shines spattered with sailboats, the Pilot Plan in the background.

August 11

Flu symptoms and my back pain are sufficient to bury my youthful fantasies. I have spent a lot of time lying down, listening to noise

106

from the neighbors and smelling the odors coming in through the window. At this age a mere flu can be fatal.

As if they were tree trunks in the middle of a powerful current, I clutch objects that are already part of me and still provoke me: Joana's clothes and a silver heart that I keep as relics, and above all photographs and more photographs that are like a summary of everything I ever was. Grafted to my body, under my skin, are the memories mixed with the remains of a daydream that I sometimes call hope and that disguises it all as a circus magician in order to fool death.

Carlos came by to visit and brought me the short story he promised. The book of thick porous pages belonged to Ana, he said. He also gave me a digital copy that I can listen to on the computer. The tone of his voice offered clear evidence of a body stooped with age.

The elderly talk about illnesses and about the advantages of youth over old age. That's not our case. Although the novelties no longer seem new to me, my instincts still retain something of my youth. As for Carlos, he was already behaving like an old man when I met him. That's why it doesn't surprise me that he defends the advantages of old age over youth.

– It's in Plato that age substitutes the pleasures of the body for those of conversation and brings a great feeling of calm and freedom. When they asked Sophocles how sexual desire evolved with age, he answered that he felt as if he had escaped from a crazy, furious tyrant; it's Plato who tells us this.

Carlos is probably right. But his philosophy, like Plato's, is of little use when I think about Joana or when Laura comes over. Age doesn't have its own virtues. It affects each person differently. It just reacts, like a chemical product, to whatever we already carry inside *ourselves, in other words, to our own defects and qualities. I didn't respond to Carlos, but I'd bet that this is in Plato too.*

– I only regret that it's precisely when we learn to live that we have to bid farewell to life, Carlos added.

[August 16]

26. Ana and her three husbands

I had moved into my studio at the end of North Wing when I got a call from the artistic director of the National Theater. She confirmed her invitation for me to document the tribute to Paulo Antonio Fernandes. Besides that, the curator of the exposition to be inaugurated at the same event wanted to see my work.

I took her my portfolios and she selected three photos from the series I'd been preparing for Eduardo Kaufman. One was of Paulo Antonio's inauguration. I went to the National Theater on the appointed day with my camera in hand. Aida was to pick me up when it was over. From there we would go out for dinner.

Stepladder paraded from one side to the other handing out smiles and greetings. Attending every reception was an ingredient in his formula for success, a formula that also included being pleasant, bragging about the things he was doing, and inventing incomprehensible concepts. It wasn't difficult to fool those who, like most of humanity, couldn't see.

Eduardo Kaufman took the floor. He spoke of social drama. Of hope. He lied with statistics. Three or four times he referred to the future and also to the memory of Paulo Antonio, the leader who had helped modernize the country. Loud applause. The photo that I took from below records the false smile etched in the corners of his mouth. It begins with long, fat legs that narrow and ends with a tiny head, a photo that I came to sell together with others of the same type, in circumstances that I will yet relate.

I was intrigued by a scene whose meaning I only came to understand days later. The congressman who had met me, Eduardo's supposed enemy, greeted him effusively. They didn't seem to exchange harsh words. They behaved like old friends.

When I saw Eduardo head toward Ana, I approached. He treated me indifferently. If he had learned of my denunciation of him to the Revenue Service, he didn't let it show.

Ana was wearing a long, dark-blue dress, cigarette in hand. She praised my photos in the exhibit and asked me to take her picture between her ex-husband Eduardo Kaufman and her current husband Carlos. All very modern, I thought, surprised as much by Ana's attitude, who seemed to have forgotten the scandal of her separation from Eduardo, as I was by Carlos's, who feigned being comfortable beside someone he had so criticized. Afterward Ana suggested I join them for a group photo that I took with the tripod using a cable release: from left to right, me, her, Carlos, and Eduardo. It's the photograph # 26 (above). In it everyone is smiling their cocktail party smiles, except me, genuinely happy to be promoted to a level equal to husband or ex-husband. I posed for posterity. I wanted a photo, as someone already said, reflecting my essence, corresponding to my neutral image and representing the person I believed myself to be. I felt my value enhanced beside Ana, noting her renewed appreciation of me.

– Dona Ana and her three husbands, I whispered in her ear.

– You, a husband? she laughed.

– What? Carlos asked.

– No, nothing, she responded and winked at me.

It took me a while to realize that neutral images don't exist, because photography captures only the passing moment, which can never be repeated.

27. The dwarf and the prophetess

When Aida arrived to pick me up as we had arranged, Iris Quelemém was leaving. I saw her against the vegetation surrounding the National Theater. Some people came up to kiss her hands. I recalled that right there many years earlier a crowd had gathered around her. Aida got out of the car and came to meet me. She wanted to see Iris up close and asked me to introduce her to the famous prophetess. I don't know whether Iris recognized me, but she was polite and mumbled something to Aida that we didn't understand. Before the Brasília sky, wide open to the whole cosmos, Aida made me promise we'd go some weekend to the Garden of Salvation.

In the center of one of the photographs I took, Iris's wrinkled brown hands squeezed the head of a child with nervous affection. In half shadow, the National Theater is a strange pyramid showing white stripes against black glass, cubes and more cubes of white on white. The prophetess, a serious face deformed by her almost ninety years, appeared in profile rickety and shrunken, being pushed in her wheelchair by a chubby dwarf wearing a brown uniform covered with ribbons and medals. I know it doesn't look good to describe someone by weight and height. But I can't find a clearer way to translate into words the image that was recorded in my brain and also in that photograph, # 27 (above).

August 17

Today the heat and dry air only became tolerable when, responding to my invitation, Mauricio and Carolina came over in the late afternoon.

Carolina arrived first. Marcela was pure joy. She began to bark as the car parked and, when my goddaughter entered the apartment, whined at length as if complaining about her long absence.

– So, how is your intern working out? Carolina asked.

– She didn't come last week. That's why I got behind on writing my book.

– She's traveling.

– If you talk to her, tell her I miss her.

– You like Laura, don't you?

I surrounded my intern with innocent adjectives and praised her qualities without indicating anything that went beyond a friendly, professional relationship, ending by explaining that I enjoyed her company.

– All the better that she plays the guitar well and reads to me.

I lied. She hadn't read anything to me, although I intend to ask her to read me the story Carlos brought over a few days ago. I prefer her voice to a talking camera. The bigger lie is that it's not Laura's absence but instead writer's block that's slowing the writing of my book. It's several times more difficult to write expecting a finished product on the first attempt, all the more so after the recent selection of photos I put together with Laura's help.

When Mauricio arrived, I asked him to open the computer file with the first of those photos.

– It should be a purple ipê tree, right at the entrance to Aida's block. Do you remember? I asked.

– I'll never forget a story you told me when I was little, Carolina said. That after creating the rainbow, God arrived with his brushes and the first things he painted in the world were the flowers. The world's colors come from them, you said. I always think about that story when I see photos of flowers.

I liked hearing her story. It reminded me that one day I had acted as a devoted, kind-hearted godfather.

We filled the rest of the afternoon with idle conversation about their activities and my inactivity. Together we solved the problems of the world, of Brazil and Brasília, I with everything I've lived through plus my skepticism, and they with their enthusiasm and critical spirit. The solutions were simple and took only a couple of hours. All around the world, we indicted egotistical countries and insane rulers. In Brazil, we changed the government. And then we ended Brasília's chaos, and I even took the opportunity to create a huge sculptural space in the Ministries Esplanade and revert to Lúcio Costa's plan to build cafés around the bus terminal.

Mauricio always gives me the impression that he still doesn't know what he'll be in life, and meanwhile music occupies all his time. If I were to call him irresponsible, I ought to apply the same adjective to myself.

He and my goddaughter left together, exactly as I'd planned. I recognize the sounds of their cars and I know that they drove away separately. Who knows, nothing prevents them from having made a date to meet later this evening. From the way they spoke they were happy to see each other.

28. The purple ipê tree

Mauricio was spending the weekend with his father. I made a drink with the vodka Aida kept in her freezer. She was there in front of me with an open book in her hands and her gestures were delicate and filled with affection. We whiled away the hours listening to music and talking, intensely interested in what each of us was saying. The night covered us with its dense, long blankets and carried us to the bottom of its black precipices. We decided to stretch it between silent stars and gusts of truth, and we heard the applause of the angels at the end of time. We were bathed more in certainty than in hope.

Aida got up to lower the blinds, wearing a thin white nightgown that revealed the outline of her body. Her undulating walk mirrored a heron's flight. I hugged her with ardor and we kissed at length.

– We waited ten years for this, she said.

– Would you have slept with me back then?

– It wasn't that I didn't want to, but I was always faithful to my husband even though he didn't deserve it.

She solemnly gave me a little gift box, with a silver heart engraved with our names inside.

Later I felt a rare sweet pleasure of lying beside her in bed. Everything happened so fast, I entered Aida with pleasure. She opened to me with the flexibility of a ballerina in a 180-degree split. The pleasure was such that when I expelled semen, saliva fell from my mouth onto her delicate skin. I ran famished eyes over her pale body, the body of someone who didn't get any sun. On her abdomen was the scar from an incision and her breasts had perhaps undergone plastic surgery.

Tears ran from Aida's eyes. They were tears of joy, she said, from thinking that that moment would never be repeated. Why not? I asked. Of course it would be repeated many, many times.

In the shower I soaped Aida's body, caressed her breasts with suds, and we slid our bodies over each other. I carefully dried each millimeter of her skin. I placed droplets of perfume behind her ears. We continued interlaced in bed not saying a word. While I was smelling her perfume, she had a sad, serene look, of a serenity and a sadness that she said were happy, the same way her tears had been happy.

– Why don't you come live with me? she suddenly asked.

I didn't answer, but the idea wasn't unappealing.

[August 19]

I started seeing Aida more often. We spoke of everything. I shared my plans and my concerns with her. On the day that I saw a list published, similar to the one I had found in one of Eduardo's computers and with the signature of the director of a state corporation, I mentioned my suspicions to her.

– If you really discovered something, give the information to the press, she suggested.

– Guga thinks so too.

The congressman I'd contacted had switched alliances, and his new party had made a deal with Eduardo's party in São Paulo. The former enemies had become campaign allies. The press, in fact, seemed a better path for my revenge.

Through Guga's contacts I got in to see a reporter from the *Correio Braziliense* and I explained to him what needed to be investigated: the slush fund from Eduardo's companies based in Amazonia, his bank accounts or those of his fronts on the Jersey or Cayman islands, the list of politicians who benefited, and the corporations participating in the scheme. My supposition, I told him, was that Eduardo Kaufman had set up a financing scheme for the mayoral election campaigns, calculating he'd receive political support when he ran for congress. He channeled his own resources and those of third parties through dummy agents. No donation was declared. I also told him about the parties Eduardo threw in Brasília financed through the same scheme.

– Illegal financing of election campaigns is quite common, he answered. But what do you have for proof? If I could at least follow some leads . . .

I showed him the two lists.

– It's a start, but it's not much, he said. Where are the bank receipts for the transfer of funds, deposits, withdrawals? Don't you have anything else? Perhaps together with these documents there's an accounting of the slush fund. If you get anything else, contact me.

I regretted not having made a complete sweep of all of Eduardo's computers. There must have been concrete proof or at least other documents that would incriminate him. At the very least there would have been dates for when the files were created.

[August 19, night]
It was June of 2001 when I was specializing in social catastrophes in Aida's company. At the movies she wanted to see por-

trayals of injustice, cruel bosses, fat cats, the wretched displaced by hunger, corrupt politicians, the drama of prostitution, and violence caused by drug trafficking. Against my will I gave in to her pleas, *reality was reality*. At the Academy we saw several films, two of them about the tragedies of the Northeast. Television actors spoke with Northeastern accents, characters sold their organs and ate lizards and cavies to survive the drought, and then emigrated to São Paulo, where they were killed in the streets or in jail . . .

One of the films was based on the autobiography of a landless peasant. Another, also autobiographical, narrated the story of a duped teenager who was taken to Spain as a prostitute.

Aida was amazed that these were true stories, that these people really existed, that the fiction wasn't fiction, that the newspaper stories could be extended in detail for two hundred, three hundred, or six hundred pages, enriched with slang, and could then be made into films.

Unlike Aida, I didn't feel the euphoria of revolt. Besides, I didn't need to show a goodness I didn't believe in. Our differences over film and religion weren't enough to keep us from being a couple in love. I wanted to be with Aida and I preferred films to attending Mass.

– Look at that purple ipê, I said.

Brasília had a thousand planters and four thousand native trees that would be covered with blooms in mid-June. One of the trees stood out, the one in the photograph above (# 28): a purple ipê, against a uniform blue of a cloudless sky. It's Aida's tree at the entrance to her block, 216 North. Together with the yellow of the *sibipiruna* trees, it adorned the sunsets, signaling winter.

– I read that the roots are so deep they reach down to the water table. That's why it's covered with blossoms even in the dry season, said Aida.

I looked to that purple ipê as a symbol of what I should do: stay deeply rooted in one place. With Aida, even if we didn't agree on everything, there was the promise of a stable relationship.

29. The ideal model or the photographer's metamorphosis

At last, after the rejections by museums and cultural centers, the gallery recommended by Tânia and which was installed in a spacious, abandoned garage in Guará finally agreed to give an exhibition of my work. Aida then tried in vain to convince me to exchange my triangles for photos that I was supposed to take in Vila Paulo Antonio. She would go with me, help me. But what was a virtue to her seemed like a flaw to me. The photos wouldn't show anything new and would be repetitive, unlike my triangles.

– Photography has to surprise, I told her.

– And you think you're surprising with this pornography?

– No one has ever made a composition of six hundred of these triangles, arranged with variations of color, tonality, and shape.

Guga, among those who didn't come to the opening reception, called to make his apologies.

– You're right to value the complicity between the photographer and his subjects. And there's no shortage of complicity in my triangle panels—I made it clear.

Ana's nephew, Termite, dropped by briefly and gave me generous praise:

– I've never seen anything like it. It was Aunt Ana who told me about the exhibition.

Nevertheless, Ana didn't come. Or Antonieta. Or even Marcela, who had agreed to be photographed for my project and for whom I had made a secret tribute, placing her triangle in the center of one of the panels. They didn't show up or make their excuses.

Antonio, who had learned about the details of the exhibition from Guga, told me on the phone:

– You never learn. Your collections are of no use at all. Nothing will ever satisfy you.

– It's like a meal, I argued. You're not satisfied once and for all. The next day you want more. And the better it is the more you want.

Veronica exhibited charm, stilettos, and a red dress. I found her crossed eyes attractive behind retro frames; they examined details of the photographs as if trying to discover secrets or make scientific analyses. Aida stayed until the end and repeated in a joking tone to those still around that she hadn't modeled for any of the photos.

When Stepladder arrived, the two photographers who were covering the opening at their own expense and at their own risk came over to take our picture. It was as if I were being recognized by an authority on photography. He didn't stay long and made no statement about my work.

My loyal friends Paulo Marcos and Tânia came.

– You don't waste any time, do you, Cadu? Tânia teased.

Unexpectedly, like a ghost that woke me from the middle of a long sleep, one of the women in the photographs appeared, with unkempt hair and beauty mistreated by time. I had met her at a moonlight party. We shared a mate gourd in a perfect blending of the Northeast—the girl was from Recife—and the pampas.

It was a cold night on an open field of the Plateau and she was wearing a Peruvian poncho. She was twenty some years old and had soft, dark skin. I took her by moonlight to a deserted spot nearby and laid the poncho on the ground. While I was savoring every millimeter of my slow delicate penetration, she yelled "no" louder each time. By her sing-song crying tone I understood the third "no" to mean "yes, enter with all the passion you can manage." I can't say that I acted like a wild animal because they don't all copulate with such energy and violence. There was a slight physical battle and, after dominating her by force, she relaxed. We made love only that one time. I'd recorded that meeting with a close-up of the triangle, the only photo in the display that was taken in the midst of such madness and with a minimum of technical resources.

I heard she'd been traumatized. If she ever saw me, she'd kill me. Now, standing in front of me, she might well be holding a grudge and a gun.

– I need to talk to you. I'll look you up at the Ministry.

Thus, she knew where to find me.

After several glasses of a terrible white wine I was going to call the reception to an end, when I learned that golden rules have golden exceptions. The exception's name was Livia and she was a colleague from work. She appeared with her green eyes and kinky hair. Her round, bulky body, plump all over and in just the right places, though unacceptable as a model, would fit right into a Renaissance painting.

– I like your nudes. Daring, sensual, creative, a bit lewd. I like them, she repeated.

I imagined her seated at her desk, naked, her hands on the computer keyboard, her derrière larger than the chair, her image forming a contrast with the frugality and sobriety of the setting.

Perhaps the sips of wine helped me say:

– The exhibition would be a thousand times better if you were covering one of my walls.

– You never asked me!

I took a photograph right there of Livia's face with my digital camera.

Later I saw myself in the left panel of a Bosch triptych being carried through the air by horrible monsters. I felt like Saint Anthony himself, the saint of temptations, hovering over scenes of punishment. It wasn't just that the golden exceptions had awakened vestiges of Christian morals in me. Those exceptions were for trivial, immature weak men. I didn't need them. The proof was that Livia had been relegated to a passing fantasy, a mere temptation confirming my transformation.

– I feel like a new man with you, I kissed Aida affectionately on the cheek. For the first time I feel satisfied with just one woman.

– You don't need to lie, she answered. I won't say that I'm not jealous. But I know how you are. I'm paying an extremely high price to be with you.

I deleted Livia's image from my digital camera and asked Aida to smile for me. Instead of using logic and reason in a torrent of words to demonstrate my affection for her, I prefer to show photograph # 29 (above), which doesn't invent or deceive, it says it all and is worth a million words. The artificial light casts a shadow of Aida on the table where a vase of flowers rests. The Venetian blinds stripe lines horizontally across the background of the picture. The emotional current that united us is visible in Aida's eyes and lips. None of my photographs, excepting one of Joana when I met her, communicates a similar feeling. It's possible to measure a woman's passion in her eyes, and there's no doubt that Aida's eyes are in love, as in love as mine at that moment.

[August 20, morning]

30. Trash on a romantic afternoon

I moved into Aida's apartment, and we created a routine for being together. We cooked. We walked around the block. We sometimes went to the interquadra bar for a beer. The bed also became a routine we never tired of. Unlike Joana, Aida wanted me. Only a few caresses were necessary to leave her wet and wild for me.

We watched television together, she, Mauricio, and I. On the news, Rio violence: the favelas of Vigário Geral, Rocinha . . . Crimes, hillside occupations by the police, their involvement in drug trafficking . . . I should dedicate my photography to crime and poverty, the only two realities, Aida insisted. Mauricio, frightened by the news, went around armed with a penknife, and if he could have, he'd have bought a gun.

– The Pilot Plan isn't Rio, Mauricio, I tried to reassure him.

One afternoon, when Aida and I were sitting on the lawn of South Lake Point, I commented:

– Mother wants me to spend more time with my brothers. But I don't have anything in common with them. They irritate me. My problem with Antonio goes way back. When we were kids he was always right. He got good grades. He already had sensible opinions.

And he turned into a serious reserved fellow, with few friends. Moderate even in drink. I've never seen him drunk. Guga, however, is a depressive intellectual. The two of them make demands of me. Antonio thinks I'm a lazy bum. Guga, that I'm stupid.

– Guga is a pompous ass, Aida answered. I don't know Antonio but, from what you say, I don't even want to meet him. He must be unbearable.

– My relationship with my mother has never been easy either. When I was a boy I provoked her to such a degree that she actually hit me. She didn't like me, at least not as much as Antonio and Guga. Antonio did everything she wanted. And Guga was an imp, he did exactly what he wanted and she never even found out.

While talking, I contorted myself to frame the photograph above, # 30. Aida is looking down toward the water or into the depths of her soul. While I was exploring her shapes, outlined in the right corner of the photograph, I saw the plastic bottles and glass shards strewn on the ground and the other pieces of trash that fill the background of the photograph and that were left, who knows, on other romantic afternoons. Aida captured my insecurity in that afternoon's transparent air. Or could she have captured it looking at my feet, more precisely at my restless tennis shoes, whose toes are visible in the foreground? She listened to me with thoughtful attention. She punctuated my sentences with deep inspiration, as one who wants to conquer fatigue and sadness. I'd never had a confidant, man or woman. With Aida beside me, I finally laid bare my defenses. Her ears cradled my fears and hesitations and my head was a dustbin of confidences.

31. The kite or the meaning of life

Aida complained of back pain as we sat at a table in an interquadra bar. Our life stories didn't need to prove anything, have a happy ending or a meaning greater than themselves. If I could only feel this very sensation from time to time, I would have clear evidence that Guga was resoundingly wrong: life was worth living. The sunny, mid-July, winter afternoon went by in several glasses of beer, sweethearts holding hands, children on bicycles, dogs beside their owners, maids, street vendors . . . Using a wide-angle lens, I took a photograph of a boy flying a kite.

That night I gave Aida a flower arrangement with carnations in the center. Antonieta and her boyfriend came over for dinner. Aida said they liked me. I saw little of them but Aida spoke often with Antonieta on the phone and they sometimes went out together.

Tânia arrived alone. The big shock for all of us that night was that she had separated from Paulo Marcos and was only just now telling us the news.

– What happened? I asked.

– Nothing. Life.

– You couldn't possibly have separated for no reason.

– My dear, anything's possible.

She didn't seem shaken by the separation. On her face she wore the joy, and sometimes also the fatigue and irritation, characteristic of the expecting. Her belly was barely noticeable. She hadn't had an ultrasound yet but she sensed it would be a girl.

– I've never seen you looking so well. You look wonderful, calm . . .

The serenity she saw in me ended when the triangle-on-the-wall-girl, the one who had contacted me at the exhibition, called in the middle of dinner. It might be blackmail, but after a week of procrastination and nights of sleeping poorly there was no way to escape.

– How did you get my phone number?

– With Aida's name from operator assistance.

I was startled. She knew too much about me, and I could already imagine her involving Aida in her blackmail. I made an appointment for the next day after work, in a corner bar at 403 South. At best, she might only want an explanation. After all, she'd never authorized me to show that photograph. Guga's argument, which I'd earlier refuted, would serve as my defense: the triangles were all the same. Despite appearances, none of them was hers.

– Who was it? Aida asked.

– A client. A sweet-fifteen birthday party.

Later, Tânia grabbed me by the arm and pulled me aside:

– I know it's early to talk about this, but I want you to be the godfather at my daughter's baptism.

She didn't mention Paulo Marcos. It was as if the child were only hers.

– And if it's a boy?

– I thought a lot about it. Boy or girl, you have to be the godfather.

That gesture of friendship was worth the sacrifice of going to church, and I was sure I'd be a good godfather.

Considering everything that had happened since I went out with Aida for our walk at South Lake Point, I thought the photo of the boy flying a kite came to define that day's atmosphere and the phase I was going through. That was the kind of photo I liked now. I had tired of taking photographs of politicians. I abandoned the triangles and scorned photographs of weddings, baptisms, or birthdays that I was taking for money.

The boy raises a kite under a blue sky. The kite soars, a four-colored diamond. The boy looks with fascination into the sky while running across the grass bordered by philodendrons and snake plants. Just as a book enlarges or shrinks according to the perceptions and imagination of the person reading it, there will be people who don't see anything but a child in that photo, a child like so many others running between apartment buildings. But there will also be someone who imagines the extraordinary lightness of the soaring kite, its graceful movement, who notices the parallelism of the primary colors between the kite and the landscape, between the diamond kite and the discernible lines drawn by the grass and the cement . . . There will also be someone who sees the joy and freedom in that boy's confident, absorbed gaze. I thought about calling that photo, # 31, simply "a happy day" or "an almost perfect day," an "almost" which I owe to the telephone call from the girl-of-the-triangle-on-the-wall.

August 21
I remember when I held Carolina on my lap, when she took her first steps, and learned her first words, when she came running with a hug as soon as she saw me, when I'd take her to the park in the block . . . Years passed—twenty years and five months to be exact—and she was here today, accompanying Laura. Marcela made a fuss over her again, this time more loudly. She gave several joyful barks and then growled as if she wanted to speak.

– *You complained so much that you were behind on your work that I decided to come help Laura, Carolina said.*

It occurred to me that Laura doesn't want to be alone with me to avoid any embarrassment.

– *I also have good news for you. A São Paulo publisher wants to make a book about Paulo Antonio and since you're considered his main photographer—those were his exact words—he wants your photos.*

My work is finally being recognized from an unexpected direction and my goddaughter is sometimes acting as my agent. She promised to help me select the Paulo Antonio photos. With a few exceptions, this part of my files hasn't been digitized yet. Many of the negatives, in some cases accompanied by contact prints, are kept in files. Among them are the ones I started to research for Eduardo Kaufman more than two decades ago.

– *You've seen a lot. You've photographed politicians. You know the behind-the-scenes version of Paulo Antonio's government . . .* Carolina said. The nervous rustling of the sheets of paper disclosed the eagerness with which she was looking through the material.

She later asked me several questions that were difficult to answer about the politics of yesterday and today. I almost thanked her for entrusting such questions to an old man like me. I couldn't answer just anything, because she valued my opinion. I remembered her mother, so passionate about politics and so sure of her points of view.

– *I can't see politics as the blue party against the red party, I answered, repeating one of Guga's opinions. What interests me is a certain way of life.*

I didn't say "yes" or "no" with regard to Paulo Antonio. And I took the opportunity to speak ill of Eduardo Kaufman.

– Have you seen Mauricio? I asked.

– To tell you the truth, no. We never run into each other.

I almost said, without beating about the bush, that Mauricio was a good catch and women don't need to wait for a man's initiative. I controlled myself. I only expressed how much I liked him.

My goddaughter said goodbye, promising to take me to a concert of a hot new band that's recreating Northeastern music.

– You're coming too, right, Laura? she proposed.

Laura promised she would, that she'd join the two of us. She found the band's songs on the Internet so I could listen to them. Then we spent the morning, she and I, trying to put the photographs in some kind of order that will help me continue my Book of Emotions. I remembered one, taken from the window of Aida's apartment that shows a fresh green spattered with the colors of the ipê.

– What an impressive memory, Laura said.

– What touches our hearts stays fixed in our memory. The rest is trash.

Laura was keenly interested in the photographs. Her voice seemed gentle and I started to smell her perfume again. It's paranoia to think she might want to abandon me.

– I don't want to hide anything from you, I said. You're going to help me choose one or two photographs from a file that I've never shown to anyone.

They were photographs of Livia.

– Don't even tell Carolina that I plan to include these photographs in the book. It will be a secret between us.

It felt good to have Laura's complicity.

– They remind me of Helmut Newton's work.

– He wouldn't have chosen such a voluptuous model.

Lastly, I asked Laura to read me the story Carlos had brought. She didn't trip over the Spanish and in a leisurely affectionate voice read the dialogue of those two characters, both named Jorge Luis Borges, a young man and an old man. They were sitting on the same bench in two different times and places, in front of the Charles River in Cambridge north of Boston, and in Geneva a few steps from the Rhône. The old man had lost his sight almost completely. Like me, he saw the color yellow, shadows, and lights. He told his other younger self what I'll repeat here: that gradual blindness is not a tragedy; it's like a slow summer sunset.

After Laura left, I still had that Northeastern music in my head and even whistled it for Marcela.

August 22

I'm not going to follow the order of the photographs I selected yesterday with Laura because, with or without photographs, I should comment on the unfolding of a story that has been pending.

[August 22]

32. Nude on the office desk and 33. Nude with earrings

– I'm desperate, the triangle-on-the-wall girl told me at the bar, two large draft beers on the table in front of us. I can't find a job. I can't stand this anymore. I desperately need money. I know you know Eduardo Kaufman. Do you think you can have him give me a job? You know it's not easy at my age.

– Right, I answered, without adding anything more than a wrinkled brow.

– I made the best of my youth. I felt free. I did whatever I wanted.

Life is beautiful, I thought, relieved to hear those sentences free of regret and above all not to see a weapon pointed at me. Happiness means escaping through one of hell's gates. The flames pushed me out the door and I left floating, as light as a balloon. We made promises. I promised that I would talk to Eduardo Kaufman, knowing that I wouldn't do it, and she promised that she'd convince a friend of hers, a journalist, to write about my photo exhibit, which I didn't believe. More than just an exchange of lies, it was one of pleasantries.

For the first time Aida asked me where I'd been and with whom. I tried to change the subject and got confused. I gave her the impression that I was hiding something and in fact I was. I wanted to spare her my explanations. Better to bury my past so that she'd be convinced once and for all that she alone completed me.

[August 22, night]

It was just my fantasy that she alone fulfilled me. When I found out Livia was moving to São Paulo, I thought first of the *flowers of renunciation,* one of my mother's inventions when I was a child. With each renunciation or sacrifice I made, my mother taught me I should add a flower to a vase. Just thinking about Livia I would have to fill several vases. It occurred to me that I could gather all those flowers and give them to Aida in the porcelain vases with beautiful shapes and gold filigree that I was building in my imagination.

Then suddenly all the vases broke at once on an afternoon that winter. I'd decided to resist temptation, except I hadn't foreseen that Livia would parade in front of me in a figure-hugging black dress.

– I'm dressed and undressed for the photographs, she said, with the nonchalance of one departing.

Saint Anthony detached himself from the monsters that carried him through the heaven of Bosch's panel and dragged himself around earth, indifferent to the scenes of punishment. Or rather I didn't think twice and, if I thought once, my anxious, confused mind barely managed to cooperate with the nervous speed of my hands. Over time, may Mother forgive me, I'd learned that renunciation and sacrifice weren't always worthwhile. "You'll be sorry someday," I heard her threatening voice and I foresaw that she was right. But better to regret lust than cowardice. And what virtue could there be in cowardice? As a professional, I shouldn't mix the act of photographing Livia with the desire I felt for her. I preferred to be unprofessional. I would pay with the price of irresponsibility, a low price for someone like me who didn't have either a career or a reputation to lose.

It was four in the afternoon and we moved upstairs. Indifferent to the risk we were running, we took photographs on the desk of the department manager atop the papers with the President's picture in the background. Should I throw caution to the wind? I did. And we stayed there a few minutes, Livia reclining over the manager's desk. Pleasure isn't measured by time but rather by intensity. Who ever said that what's done in a hurry can't be delicious?

We heard footsteps. I sat at the desk. Livia didn't want to stop. She knelt and lowered her lips between my legs. I closed my eyes (may God protect us). I know I shouldn't insert God in the story. It would actually be: may Violeta protect us! She simply opened the door, apologized, and left, unperturbed.

I developed the photographs and sent them to Livia—two of them are reproduced above. She was recorded in those photographs like a butterfly that embellished an afternoon. She passed through my garden flapping her wings and flew away. Perhaps she'd never return.

34. Partial view of happiness on an August day

A few days later, a Sunday, Aida suggested:

– Let's go to the Garden of Salvation. I want to see my future.

I agreed. I wanted to see my future too. I wanted to see our future together.

Mauricio went with us and, already at the entrance to the Garden, he was blown away by the altar containing oriental images and the figure of a bearded, white-haired black man.

– This is Father Joãozinho of Angola, said a vestal virgin in a shy voice and fluttering dress of blue tulle.

I identified myself. My connections with the Garden of Salvation had been good for something, and particularly my feigned interest in the medium who was a professor of theology, the one who preached that chance didn't exist and that everything, absolutely everything, was ordained until the end of time. He called me "brother" and "friend" and helped us be received by the Prophetess Iris Quelemém. We were taken to the worship hall where we should wait.

– We're open to many divinities, preached a man in a brown uniform covered with medals and crossed with yellow and red sashes indicative of his hierarchical degree. Our philosophy particularly welcomes mediumistic religions: Allan Kardec's

Spiritism, Umbanda, Candomblé, the Eclectic Spiritualist Universal Fraternity, the Valley of the Dawn, the Religion of God and even others, like Santo Daime and the Union of the Vegetable. What we have in common is the recourse to mediums as a means to the relationship of possession, a sacred relationship that enables the embodiment of the spirits of gods and men in agents like us. Any questions?

– Allow me to say that I'm Catholic, Aida explained.

– It's possible to be Catholic and attain the spirituality of this Garden. In fact, many who come here are Catholic. Others belong to Protestant or Evangelical denominations, including the Pentecostals. And people from other Christian sects that are neither Catholic nor Evangelic, like Jehovah's Witnesses, Mormons, and Seventh-Day Adventists, come here too.

Aida wanted to see the surgery room. Several chairs were set out in a semicircle in the "hospital" anteroom, where patients waited for a medium through whom a famous doctor would operate without incisions.

At last, Iris received us.

– Human interference in the heavenly bodies, she told us, can alter destinies foreseen by astrology. Men are able to send spaceships to destroy comets tens of millions of kilometers from earth. One day they'll yet alter the orbits of other celestial bodies.

Then she took Aida to a small, dark room.

– You're going through an ascendant phase in your professional activity and you'll be successful in your plans for the future, she saw in her crystal ball. Your story on earth isn't finished yet. You have living to do. In matters of love, with perseverance and wisdom, minor disturbances will be fleeting. They'll culminate in a fullness never before achieved. Each person's mission has a time to be completed; some are completed during their lifetimes, others only many years after they've died, sometimes even centuries later. That's why I advise you to do what you believe in and deem necessary, calmly and without deadlines.

When Iris received me she passed on teachings that could be summed up this way: suffering is worthwhile. I liked believing in those teachings although I only came to understand them much later. Looking into her crystal ball, she prophesized:

– Your son will unite the two of you. He needs you. He'll be a source of worries and also of great joys. And he'll help you both in your old age.

Mauricio had remained seated on a sofa outside. Iris hadn't said "Aida's son" or, by mistake, "your son with Aida," just "your son." The comment could only apply to Bigfoot, my son with Berenice. Finally, she commanded:

– Look straight ahead without fear.

Straight ahead I didn't see anything other than her wrinkles and still some doubts. I didn't believe she had foreseen the future, but she certainly reminded me that it existed and that part of it was up to me.

I left with two resolutions. The first was that I should meet Bigfoot. The second left me euphoric. The time had arrived to propose to Aida. As Guga would say with his erudite quotations, the reason was *simply simple*; if we liked each other so much, why not marry her and make it official like my parents and Antonio had done, as Mother had always demanded?

That night, Aida and I made love as if we'd been married for forty years. By this I'm not saying that it was boring, unimaginative sex.

It was good in that there was no anxiety or urgency in our movements and that our bodies knew each other, adjusted to each other, fitting perfectly and comfortably like two magnets attracting. We stayed that way until sleep came over us and each rolled to one side. I couldn't consider the relationship with Aida a wild passion. It was a friendship with sex, the tranquil marriage in pastel colors that I had always wanted and that contrasted with my troubled past and gaudy colors in Joana's company.

The day dawned and the great kiskadee sang continuously: "kiska-dee?" From the window of Aida's apartment a vibrant green, spattered in purple by the ipê, shone with the first rays of sun. That's when I took photograph # 34.

[August 23]

35. Fixations number 1

In August of 2001 I received a note from the triangle-on-the-wall girl at my work address, together with a newspaper article. She had fulfilled her part of our deal. A critic had written about my exhibition. I wanted to believe that the opinions of others didn't matter but suddenly they mattered a great deal, regardless of whose opinions they might be, even a critic's, just one inarticulate and despicable critic who was incapable of understanding the deepest meanings of my work and who, probably moved by envy, wrote for a newspaper no one ever read. If those words had just been spoken to me, they would have gone in one ear and out the other. But written text, if it escapes the trash, can be viewed forever, like a photograph, and end up being confused with reality.

We know mankind's first sentiment was pride; the second, vanity. We're capable of killing over such nonsense. I use the royal "we" so that my defects are transformed into an excusable human characteristic. I must admit, my pride and my vanity were wounded. I wanted my work to seduce, surprise, and shock. Suddenly my critic considered it tedious, graphic, and vulgar, in addition to not at all original. Indifference and silence would have pained me less than that cruel attention to my work.

I reproduce (above) one of the panels from the exhibition so that it can be judged with impartiality and objectivity, although, for that, one would have to imagine it a hundred times larger.

[August 23, afternoon]

36. Happy couple

I had a nightmare. The vestal virgin that we'd met at the entrance to the Garden of Salvation was brought to me by Mauricio. A thorn had entered her body right above the vulva. She asked me to help her remove it. I looked. She was wearing nothing under her petticoat. She had no pubic hair. And her whole body was milky white. I took her to the temple in Aida's car, looked in vain for a place to park and ended up leaving it in a no-parking area. Next we walked holding hands, crossed a glass-covered bridge alongside the crowd, and then I was the one who was naked. We slipped on the soapy floor, I didn't know where we were going to stop and I worried that Aida and Mauricio could see us through the glass. I awoke relieved that it was only a dream.

I called Antonio:

– I think I'm going to get married.

– You'll like it. It's never too late to have children.

– It's not children I'm thinking about—and I almost told him that I already had a son.

Antonio was right in fact; I'd never feel fulfilled until I could be a father to someone, and I couldn't say I'd been a father to Bigfoot. But Aida didn't need to conceive another child, I could adopt Mauricio. Or, who knows, I could approach Bigfoot and acknowledge paternity. Only a biological son would transmit my genes to future generations.

Since Antonio wanted to meet Aida, my phone call resulted in an invitation for one of his Sunday lunches.

– So, when's the wedding? he asked us as soon as we arrived.

– Things are fine the way they are. We're not thinking about that, Aida answered.

I hadn't gotten up the courage to make my intention lead to a marriage proposal and, faced with Aida's answer, I preferred to keep quiet when faced with Antonio's look of interrogation and censure.

When we sat down at the table, he wanted to know about my participation in the tributes to Paulo Antonio Fernandes, the reason for my coming to Brasília. I told him my problems with Eduardo Kaufman.

– Opportunistic s.o.b., Veronica said.

– Don't be such an extremist. You always think all politicians are opportunists, Antonio answered.

– Yes, I'm an extremist. There isn't a single one who's any good. This Eduardo, besides being an opportunist, pays for the politicians' orgies.

– You've made up your mind: No one in the world is any good.

That small disagreement was enough to set Antonio and Veronica off into an elaborate demonstration of their methods of warfare. They were explosive, sparks flying in the form of a word, an unspoken word, a glance, a missed glance. Both of them felt offended for no apparent reason and claimed that the other one was too touchy about innocent comments.

Aida seemed shocked by the way the two of them were behaving. My nephews, also at the table, said nothing.

– This interests me. Are you sure that Eduardo finances these parties? I asked Veronica, indifferent to the conjugal battle.

– They say he does, you know? Apparently he uses an escort service.

I remembered the site I'd consulted in the apartment at 104. The indications of Eduardo's involvement were clear: Veronica had heard about it . . . and there was the evidence of the sites he logged onto on the computer. Maybe Akiko, the Japanese girl who appeared on the site, the champion of page hits on Eduardo's computer, could one day be useful.

– You two make such a cute couple! Veronica said, offering to take my photo with Aida, the one seen above, a smiling photograph of our faces touching.

I feel enormous affection for that photograph that I didn't take and I prefer it to any wedding photo. For the tenderness of our expressions, it's the best of all of the photos of me with Aida. Anyone studying it objectively—even Veronica herself, who took it, couldn't see its value. There are photographs that have only subjective value, sometimes for the person who took them and in this case for the subject, like the page of a diary that records what moved us deeply and whose dimensions only we understand.

Several days later I put that photo in a frame and gave it to Aida as a gift. Without thanks or comment she placed it on the bedroom dresser and said:

– I need to talk to you. It's very serious.

What could it be? She seemed depressed, pale, as if she were still in shock from suddenly hearing some terrible news. Could somebody have told her about Livia and me? I couldn't allow some nonsense named Livia to destroy the image of happiness printed on that photo on the dresser. I thought about telling her everything, feigning profound regret. I say "feigning" because if, on the one hand, Livia had added above all a certain uneasiness to my triangle collection, on the other I didn't feel anything approaching regret, much less profound regret.

– Aida, I know it doesn't matter to you, but it does to me. I'd like you to agree to be my wife. For us to get married in church and a civil ceremony, the way it should be. Look at this photo, it doesn't lie: we're a happy couple.

Aida began to cry. She wept.

– We'll talk later. I want to be alone, she said, sobbing.

Mauricio came into the bedroom. Aida hugged him, still crying.

August 28

When Mauricio arrived this morning I hugged him, remembering the hug that Aida had given him two decades ago. He came at my request to help me organize the photos of his mother. Even when I could see I never wanted to revisit them, but of all the photographs they're the clearest in my memory.

He was upset by some violent scene he'd witnessed.

– Do you remember when you used to carry a pocketknife and I told you Brasília wasn't Rio? Today I'd say you're right, I said.

I asked if he'd seen Carolina. No, he hadn't. I tried to tell him how much alike they are. They have the same sensitivity and the same interests: I mentioned my goddaughter's intelligence and musical taste.

– She doesn't play an instrument like you do but she knows how to appreciate good music.

I described a concert she'd taken me to a few days ago. In short, I left Mauricio with the most vivid impression of my goddaughter.

By chance he met Laura, who raved about me and described the work she's been doing here. How wonderful that Laura sings my praises!

In my future, two little lights shine. One, with a new glow, is named Laura. The other has a persistent, yellowish old-fashioned glow. It's Joana. They're distant stars. But I can still see them.

The tiny future stars dazzled me so much that I almost gave up organizing Aida's photographs. I realized my error in time. That would be abandoning what was so dear to me for an unattainable future. I don't want to cure the pain of yesterday with today's fantasies. I'll never forget Aida. Mainly, I'll never forget those days of waiting and agony.

I dictated the files corresponding to Aida's photos to Mauricio. I renumbered some of them. They'll serve as an outline for whatever I write over the next few days. I continue to avoid showing Mauricio what I've already written. I fear that our memories don't coincide and that when he reads certain passages he'll think I'm trying to improve my own image in his eyes, feigning an amiability that I don't actually feel. But when I finish I'll ask him to edit my Book of Emotions. I want him to improve the writing and if he doesn't like the content, I hope he'll forgive me. I haven't included and I won't include anything more than what was lived. Less, yes. Words to describe profound pain will always be insufficient.

– Laura's right, Mauricio told me. You never forget an image.

– I do too, many of them. But I don't forget you or your mother.

Now that he's left, I'm updating my diary on the computer and writing a few more pages in my Book of Emotions. *I served myself a glass of wine. The ethanol odor of the cars filling the streets enters through the window. It's a good thing I don't drive and almost never leave home.*

The helicopters leave the sky confused. I manage to neutralize their noise listening to Cole Porter with the volume turned up. Marcela's at my feet and by the way she rests her head on my shoes, I know she's happy with my musical choice.

[August 29]

37. Anguish disguised in bowling balls

– I should have told you before, Aida said, a few hours after her fit of sobbing. I acted selfishly. I thought I'd live at least a few happy days before I die. The doctors give me six months at most.

It was a cancer that had been detected too late. It had already metastasized.

I didn't know what to say. I hugged her for minutes that lasted an eternity and later tried to cheer her up:

– You're tough. You'll come out of this.

– No. There's no hope. The doctors have already given me the bad news.

– Whatever happens, I'll be right beside you. I'll take care of you.

– Promise that you'll take care of Mauricio?

– I'll take care of you and him.

I felt good being loving, useful, and mainly honest, with a purpose in life. It was good to show that I was good. To feel good. To be good. Good was right and right was good.

I invited Mauricio to go bowling. We went in Aida's car to the Parkshopping Mall. We stayed there late, concentrating on the game, not saying a word. That's where the photo above is from, # 37. It's not for the good composition or the pleasing way I framed the bowling balls that this photograph deserves to be reproduced here. It could well be confused with a good advertisement. But it's special to me, because the shock I felt is engraved in it. Never had a piece of news taken the ground out from under my feet and undone my horizons like this one. I could write an entire book about how a disease can interrupt our calculations, plans, and foresight, destroy the meaning of the story we were writing on earth, and leave us adrift, bewildered in the face of the unexpected and unjust. Aida never left my thoughts, which came and went, associated with the bowling balls. *Life is just what happens to you while you're busy making other plans.*

38. Mauricio thinking of Sharon Stone

– I brought a film with a gorgeous, totally naked woman, I told Mauricio the next day. A film I hadn't seen in years.

We went out for a walk around the block. I showed him a guava fruit at the top of the guava tree. The branch as hard as glass broke under Mauricio's weight. I took him home and patiently applied dressings to his injured arm. It was the first time I had been a nurse or even taken care of someone.

I kissed Mauricio's scalp. I didn't say that what was happening to him and his mother was divine injustice only because I didn't believe in God.

– And your homework, have you done it?

– No. I don't want to today. Let's watch the film you brought.

It was hard to imagine that Aida would die, but if it happened, I would indeed take on the responsibility of raising Mauricio, even if that meant I'd have to redouble my efforts to earn a living. My love for Aida would live on in my dedication to Mauricio. That could be my mission in life. I hoped to live long enough to see him become an accomplished adult.

The afternoon sun invaded the living room. Thick, black eyebrows delineated Mauricio's thin, dark face. I recorded in the photograph above, # 38, a gleam in his eyes and the spontaneous laugh of someone who's happy at the possibility of seeing Sharon Stone naked. In that look and that laugh, I saw another possibility, dear and sublime: I'd be a real father to Mauricio, taking him to school every day, helping him with his homework, playing with him, and watching movies together.

*

[August 30]

39. Spaceship with crown of thorns

The same barren fields, the same esplanades, the same park that earlier wore vibrant, varied colors had acquired a sepia tone. I'd be alone in the world. It was one more reason to take photographs. When taking photographs I felt accompanied, I didn't know yet by whom. But one day I'd show those photographs or those photographs would show themselves.

Brasília sizzled like a pan. I wandered aimlessly, stooped with sadness. The series of photos of cracked sidewalks came from that period. Tufts of grass emerged from some of the cracks. From others only red clay was visible.

From one of the cracks I picked up the cellophane wrapper of an empty cigarette carton. I was playing with it between my fingers, not paying attention to it or to myself. A living photo played out before me: starving boys, expectant mother, perfect framing of social drama. Now another approached, it looked like a Cartier-Bresson, a girl jumping a water puddle, still suspended in air while the expression of the elderly in the background was one of pain and uneasiness. The moments were fleeting. The photographs vanished. The faces of the elderly were now expressionless. The girl, with her back to me, was swinging her flowered dress in the direction of an apartment block.

An unknown gringo appeared. You know a gringo by the movement of his lips, a rhythmless body, and by the style and size of the shoes. I waited until those shoes took long strides across the background composed of trash thrown on the grass at the edge of the curb, the dry leaves, pieces of styrofoam, perforated paper, cigarette butts, a popped balloon, aluminum foil sparkling in the sun, cardboard, broken roof tiles . . . I threw the cellophane I was still carrying in my hand on top of that trash. A photograph of what? I didn't know. A photo of a recognizable long stride atop abandoned refuse.

I walked several more kilometers, sweating my shirt and my thoughts through those repetitive interquadras, with their "air of elegant monotony," as someone famous said. "Man's eye serves as a photograph of the invisible, just as the ear serves as an echo for silence," I remembered the complete sentence quoted by my brother Guga. The landscapes repeated themselves as in Ravel's *Bolero*, blocks and more blocks, highway cloverleaves and more cloverleaves, until the clouds bled in the late afternoon sky.

I walked down in the direction of the Esplanade. I contemplated the human creation as if it were divine, the anti-city, symbol and desire, that came to humanize the Central Plateau; technique in search of beauty, as Niemeyer said. I had already seen those buildings thousands of times, but I was seeing them anew. In the foreground, the baptistry in the shape of a spaceship transported me to a strange faraway world where Aida's voice resounded softly in the midst of the thick fog and disappeared little by little. But I saw her hands crossed over her chest holding a red rose I'd given her. She was pale and her eyes were closed. I did the framing for photo # 39 (above), its metallic colors emphasized by the Cibachrome print. Behind the baptistry the cathedral rose like a crown of thorns. I didn't believe in God, but there I rendered my soul unto Him.

[August 30, night]

40. Mysterious writing

I continued walking, now in the direction of the South Wing. The enormous square, with no trees or fountains, an immensity of stones and concrete, was spattered with street vendors, neckties and more neckties hanging on a line, a rational and surreal landscape right in the midst of Banking Sector South. The ruins of the modern were the ruins of my dreams.

Later, in front of Block E at 102 South, an abandoned square, some benches, not a soul. I sat down. The hopelessness of a failed life descended over me. I felt defenseless before the cruel world. I cried for the first time since I had returned to Brasília. I wasn't crying for Aida. I was crying for myself. I was crying for the fact that in losing her I'd lost the best thing I had achieved over the past few years or perhaps in my entire life: some sense of dignity and the expectation of unwavering love.

I noticed the sign: "Jesus, the only salvation." Me, entering a church? I'd never do that. I read it again: "Jesus, the only salvation." No harm could come to me. I went in.

On the door, another sign: "Worried about tomorrow? About the job shortage? Love?" Below, the answer read: "But seek ye first the kingdom of God, and his righteousness; and all these things shall be added unto you. Take therefore no thought for the morrow: for the morrow shall take thought for the things of itself. Sufficient unto the day is the evil thereof. (Matthew 6: 33-4.)"

– Brother, you look like you need help, said a well-dressed woman, with straight black hair down to her waist. She was carrying a Bible in her hands.

I said nothing.

– The Lord is always aware of our problems. He helps those who want to be helped, she continued.

I kept silent.

– If you need to, you can come to us any time, day or night, the woman went on, handing me a card with phone and fax numbers and email addresses.

Dazed, I put the card in my pocket.

The light coming through the large windows around the curved walls made patterns in the shape of hieroglyphs that I was meant to interpret. It was mysterious writing, made for me, that can be seen in the photo above. There are three lacy gray bands climbing the pale blue wall where I read a trace of hope. Aida had faith. Faith could move mountains, miracles were possible for special people, and there was no one in the world with more faith or who was more special than Aida.

August 31, late at night

Today when Laura arrived, Marcela jumped up and made a fuss over her. Laura then told me she'd been introduced to the other, first Marcela.

– When she found out I knew you, she didn't even hide her joy from her husband. She said she'd been your girlfriend, right in front of him.

By the expression she used, "girlfriend," it's clear that she has good memories of me. It's fair to include a few more lines about her in my Book of Emotions, *although what's worth telling is not supported by my old diary, which I had already completed when we started seeing each other again, or by any of the photographs, unless I can locate a certain photograph of an empty bed.*

– She's still a vigorous woman. Thin. A nervous way of speaking, restless eyes. She told me herself that she's new and improved after several plastic surgeries and a complete regeneration treatment.

– She didn't need those things to keep herself young. She can't be more than fifty years old.

– She wanted to know if you were married, if you had children. I told her you had a dog.

– I hope you didn't tell her the name.

– I left it for her to discover.

Marcela breathed deeply as if she understood.

I never attained the same degree of freedom to talk about myself with anyone else as I have with Laura. May her internship last forever! It will be a way to inject myself with doses of youthfulness each time she comes.

She helped me find one more photo of the purple ipê for my book, and another of Antonieta lying on the bed with Aida.

– She was a friend of ours, a gorgeous woman, I explained.

I called her attention to the boy with sad eyes, leaning out the window.

– It's Mauricio on the day of my marriage to Aida.

– May I print it? she asked and told me she's seen Mauricio once in a while. She said nothing more, nor did I ask.

[September 2]

41. Spring sacrifice

Upon seeing the card on my night table, Aida wanted to know what church it was from. I told her about the sign that read "Jesus, the only salvation" and everything else that had happened.

– It may be a call, a warning.

Two days later she repeated that same impression. I remember the date well because it was September 11 and Paulo Marcos called me to discuss the scenes of horror on television. We went out with Carlos and Ana to an interquadra bar.

– This is of no importance to us, Paulo Marcos observed.

– It ends up affecting everyone, my friend, mainly because they've decided it's a war. This will end up creating more terrorists, more resentment, the cells will reproduce on their own all over the place, in the Middle East, Europe, the U.S., Carlos ventured.

– It's intolerance against intolerance, Ana said.

I was living my own September 11, and I decided to call one of the numbers on the card. I explained Aida's situation, asked if they'd see non-members of the church and off we went the following Sunday.

In the temple, a roughly sixty-year old Pernambucan stonemason confirmed that when he was possessed by the devil he pounded on the walls, rolled on the ground, and hurt himself all over.

– But ever since Jesus freed me from drugs and liberated me from Satan, he declared, I dedicate myself to only two things: my family and the church. I bear this witness to the honor and glory of merciful Jesus.

A woman took the floor to talk about her marriage:

– When I met my husband, he had just been saved by the Lord after spending more than twenty years living as an outcast. I didn't believe in religion. Soon I was baptized, descending into the waters beneath the fire of the Holy Spirit. If today I've found and love Jesus, it was for the love of my husband.

The story of a middle-aged man caught our attention:

– Three years ago I had been diagnosed with an incurable lung cancer. After several sessions in our church, the doctor who had told me there was no hope confirmed that the tumor had disappeared and he never understood how the God of the Impossible saved me.

Afterward we watched a cleansing session. Those present moved their arms, yelled phrases in unison, and some of them went into a trance. A bishop dressed in white took the head of one of the possessed women in his hands and moved it from side to side. That's how the ceremony of liberation began. The prayers to stimulate the manifestation of the devil grew to a crescendo, accompanied by the solemn timbres of an electric piano. Those present spun around with their eyes closed, with their hands crossed and placed over the top of their heads. After that they threw their hands first in the direction of the possessed woman and then backwards.

– What's your name, demon? the bishop repeated the question several times, until she answered almost incomprehensibly, with an angry guttural voice:

– Exu.

– Who else? Are you alone? Are any other demons present?

– I'm alone, the woman answered.

– What is your name, Exu?

– Exu Skull.

– What have you done to this poor woman, Exu Skull?

– I'm taking her to perdition.

– She's not to blame for this. It's Exu who's inside of her. What do you think? Can Jesus save her from this Satan?

– Yes, he can, the crowd answered.

– Do you think she can be saved? Yes or no?

– Yes, they all answered.

– In the name of Jesus, leave this woman's body, the bishop said, placing his hands on her head. He repeated it several times, raising his voice:

– Out, out, in the name of Jesus. I want you to help me and to pray with me: "Out, out, out."

The crowd yelled in a chorus, all raising their hands and then throwing them back:

– Out, out, out.

The woman opened her eyes, as if she were suddenly coming to.

– Are you feeling all right? the bishop asked.

– Yes.

– Thank the Lord.

– Thank the Lord, they repeated.

Aida watched everything very calmly, but she didn't want to submit to that ritual. The bishop gave her a white ribbon with the inscription *Father of Lights*, for her to tie around her wrist while she mentalized the evil from which she wished to be liberated. He blessed us with a branch of rue and gave us fluidized water.

– Put these portions of salt on the table or in the corners of the apartment. This rue soap is to rid the body of impurities and this bottle of oil is to repel the evil eye.

I don't know how much faith Aida placed in that. But she told me that she would use the soap and the bottle of oil.

When we got home, I noticed that the acacias painted the rear of the block yellow and the leaves of the sapucaia-nut tree had changed from green to purple. Another brighter purple appeared on the ipê that had flowered as was to be expected in the month of September. For someone who doesn't know my story, photograph # 41 of that purple ipê against a smooth bright blue sky seems innocent and happy. But when we reached the block that Sunday, Aida's tree, the one I had selected as a symbol of who I should be and that I was now photographing, seemed sad and unhappy, signifying sacrifice and death.

[September 4]

42. Landscape, its hidden meanings

Ana invited me to her birthday party. Not knowing about Aida's illness, she asked me to pass along the invitation to her as well. I didn't do it so as not to irritate her. Even if she were healthy she'd never accept an invitation from Ana. I went alone, with no guilt, because I felt tired; I deserved to surround myself with joy, and I had the right to a break from my dedication to Aida.

I competed with my brother Guga for a dance with Tânia, and my persistence was rewarded. While Guga sniffed coke and, being a great dancer, was inevitably successful with all the available girls, I concentrated on Tânia. Her still recent pregnancy didn't diminish her vitality and added a radiant beauty to her face.

– I had an ultrasound. It's a girl, she told me.

I started to think that I could be more than a godfather, a father, to that child. Better than acknowledging a son who had become a criminal. I ended up dancing with Tânia until very late. I hadn't had so much fun in a long time.

When I got home Aida was sleeping with Antonieta by her side. As I took their photograph I managed to wake them. That's the only photograph I've ever taken of Antonieta. Ever since she avoided meeting me at the Water Hole Park, I had never been relaxed around her, not even after she'd started to spend a lot of time in our apartment. She talked to me as if nothing had happened between us. It was better that way. In fact, little had happened outside my imagination, which after flying so high had its wings clipped.

– Where have you been? Aida asked me, when Antonieta left.

– I went out to take photographs.

It wasn't a complete lie. I carried the camera over my shoulder and had taken a photo of Tânia.

– At this hour? She must have noticed I smelled of alcohol.

The next day Ana called her to say she was sorry about her illness and, without meaning to, gave me away. I could never forget Aida's sad eyes that day staring out one of her apartment windows as if she were thoroughly analyzing the distant landscape made up of hills, similar to the ones I'd photographed on the day of my imaginary walk with Antonieta in the Water Hole Park, the place where I had met Tânia too. I set the camera on the tripod and used the zoom. A tiny plane crossed the horizon. What can be seen beyond the hills and beneath the camera is what makes that photo dear to me. It looked like a landscape before the storm or already in the eye of a hurricane. Even so, it calmed me and enveloped my mistakes in beauty, because in the green and blue layers of the far-off hills the landscape was created out of the shapes and colors of doubt, promise, frustration, guilt, and also love.

September 4
The pleasure of dancing with Tânia, which had been so great, ended right there, in that pre-dawn, but the guilt remains with me today because it's the nature of pleasure to be fleeting while guilt is intractable.

So many are the names of pain—abandonment, egotism, scorn, bitterness... With Marcela here by my side, I'll be forgotten. If anyone remembers me, let it be for the loves I've had, all so different one from another. All of them, loves.

September 5
Today I drank half a bottle of red wine. I gave up drugs and distilled alcohol long ago. In old age, the body can't handle them. Red wine doesn't always agree with Brasília's temperature but disagreements have their merits. I offered Laura a glass. She doesn't drink. Or smoke.

Together we reviewed at least three years. I asked her to choose a photograph of Antonio, Veronica, and the children, as well as a series taken in Vila Paulo Antonio, of which I have vivid memories.

Today Vila Paulo Antonio is one of the most violent towns in the vicinity of Brasília. A few years ago my photographs were requested for a book about its "before and after." The "before" I thought was dull, ugly, and squalid. Over time, the dull, ugly, and squalid were carried by progress to greater lengths and to an even higher degree of misfortune. The streets I photographed, whose beaten earth preserved a certain rural dignity, were poorly dressed in potholed asphalt and cheap commerce, like a naked Indian who left the jungle to become shabby in the city.

– Have you seen Mauricio? I asked Laura.

– Regularly. We even met yesterday.

– He's abandoned me.

– He adores you. He'll never abandon you.

I get the impression that they're dating. This doesn't surprise me but it's annoying, because I still want Carolina to be the chosen one. In my duty as godfather, I'll do anything within my power for that to be the outcome.

The dating theory annoys me for another reason too. No matter how inopportune and even absurd it might be to think this way, it's as if I were losing Laura to Mauricio. I sent him an email. Why has he disappeared?

September 7

I wrote a little every day during precisely three months. I don't know if I'll have the energy to keep up this pace.

Today is Independence Day, and they're celebrating my national virtues and defects in the street. On the computer I heard the description of the military parade being broadcast on a television channel. I also listened to a speech about everything the country has accomplished in the world: industry, agriculture, space . . . Praise and more praise for the technological advances . . . I didn't get all choked up. I prefer moral and political advances. My patriotism never went beyond the attempt to destroy Eduardo Kaufman, a cancer in our political culture.

To tell the truth, I haven't even decided whether I'm for or against national borders. I learned a lesson in world politics: sometimes those who defend borders want to perpetuate injustice and mediocrity, while those who favor abolishing borders are certain to be the invaders.

September 7, afternoon
The first photograph, taken by Niépce, is the same age as independent Brazil: it's from 1822 and shows a table set outdoors, trees in the background. This thought came to me for no particular reason, but gives me the excuse to join the street party. I commemorate the birth of photography.

[September 10]
43. No more no less

When Mauricio noticed the dishes of salt distributed in the corners of the apartment, I had a frank conversation with him.

– I prefer to tell you that your mother is suffering from a serious illness . . .

– I know. She has cancer, right?

I hugged Mauricio.

– I don't want to live with my father. I want to live with you.

– I promise that I'll always be with you. Or better yet, you'll come live with me.

– Father doesn't want me to. He wants me to live with him.

– We'll see. We'll figure it out.

The first step would be to marry Aida. She was divorced, she could get married. I returned to that subject.

– I don't want you to marry me out of pity, she said.

– I want to marry you because I love you. I had already proposed.

– Before you knew about my illness.

– That doesn't change my decision.

I collected the necessary paperwork. I wanted the wedding to take place promptly and to be married under the system of separation of property, so Aida's family wouldn't think that I intended to make a claim to the inheritance. Her siblings were limited to three pale sisters, two older and one younger than Aida, who had arrived from Goiânia and were camped in our apartment.

In a matter of days I convinced the justice of the peace and the priest to come to our house for the ceremonies. The civil ceremony, followed by the Catholic one. Tânia and Paulo Marcos, still separated, Antonieta with her boyfriend, and Aida's sisters were the only people present. Tânia, contemplative in her austere beauty, was the matron of honor in the Catholic ceremony.

Aida's joy, aided by make-up and the vibrant yellow of her dress, overrode the effects of the disease. I don't want to dwell here on the description of the rain that seemed to sprinkle that happy September afternoon with sadness. The Northeasterners had brought the term "cashew rains" for those few sudden showers that coincided with the start of the flowering of the cashew trees.

– You'll take good care of Mauricio? Aida asked me again.

– I'm not just going to take care of him. I'm going to adopt Mauricio. Legally. I've already started the legal procedures.

I took a photo of Mauricio, thoughtful and reclined against the window before the civil ceremony got under way. One foot against the wall, uncombed hair, he looks at the camera with doubt and distrust. He's wearing a shirt with long, wide sleeves and has his hands in his pockets. There are photos that only acquire their full significance when compared with others of the same subject. Such is the case of this one when contrasted with photograph # 15. Mauricio now has an adolescent air about him, and not only because of his height. He had matured in a matter of months. A photo is measured also by its ability to portray its subject in the truest, most accurate manner. For me, photograph # 43 above is absolutely faithful; it is Mauricio himself at that moment, no more no less.

[September 10, late afternoon]

44. Aida, Mauricio, and me

– Why don't we go to the Garden of Salvation? I proposed to Aida, remembering the surgery room and the medium, the professor of theology who already considered me a friend.

Through him, I was able to schedule Aida's operation for a few days from then, cutting into an enormous waiting list.

– May I go too? Mauricio asked when we were about to leave.

– No. This time you'd better not. It may take a while. Stay with your aunts, Aida said. Besides, your father is coming by here today.

Mauricio scowled.

I couldn't find the one photograph that I had taken on that trip to the Garden of Salvation. If I find it, it will have the # 44. And if I don't find it, too bad! There are facts I need to narrate, with or without a photograph.

In the operating room, when a priestess learned that Aida suffered from an incurable cancer, she was categorical in her claim:

– There are no incurable diseases. At least not here.

She told the story of a terminal cancer patient who had started to recover right there after the operation by the medium. Aida's surgery would take place without cutting. Energy would pass through the medium's hands to her body like a miraculous chemotherapy.

Aida felt unwell. She became dizzy.

– It's the heat, I told her.

– I want to leave.

– Just a little longer, until the medium arrives.

If only one person believes in something impossible, like water turning into wine and wine into blood, he's considered crazy. But if there are many, they depart the realm of madness for the realm of religious faith. If for Aida and a significant portion of humanity Jesus Christ was born to a virgin, resurrected from the dead and risen to heaven, if he could be eaten in the form of a thin round wafer and if some words spoken over a wine from California, Burgundy, or the São Francisco Valley, transformed it into the blood of that same Christ, why couldn't she trust the healing powers of the invisible scalpel?

A blue sash crossed the medium's khaki clothes. In front of him, a woman knelt. He placed his hands on her head:

– Without faith the energy won't work. Have faith and you will be cured.

A beam of light entered the dark room through the glass roof like a divine message. Aida became solemn. Her fragility was obvious. She felt something that she later described only as "undefinable" when the medium placed his hands on her.

It was her last chance. For this reason I promised the gods and all the spirits of the Garden of Salvation that I'd believe in them and adore them for the rest of my life, visiting churches, temples, pyramids, and macumba yards, if Aida were saved. This was blackmailing the heavens, trying to bargain with the divinity, but at that moment not only did my coin of exchange seem acceptable to the gods, but I was also under the impression that at least one of them had heard me, because Aida's mood improved.

When we got back to the apartment, we ran into Mauricio's father.

– I need to talk to you, alone, he said to me.

We went to the building entrance. He confronted me with his furious eyes:

– You're a pervert! You keep showing Mauricio pornographic videos.

– Me?

– Don't try to deny it, he told me himself. And if you don't get out of here now, I'll go to court to take Mauricio immediately. I didn't want to do this now because he's company for Aida. But you leave me no alternative.

Tall, with light curly hair and a hook nose, he had twice the muscles I had. Better to let him win the verbal battle and for me to stay with Aida and Mauricio. In fact, he missed both targets: he didn't manage to expel me from the apartment or take Mauricio; but without realizing it, he hit a third target: he made me give up the adoption process.

– What did he want? Aida asked.

– Nothing, I answered. Forget it! I want to take a photo of the three of us.

It's the only one in which just the three of us—Aida, Mauricio, and I—appear. I took it with the automatic shutter. Mauricio is sitting on Aida's lap, on the bed; I'm alongside hugging her. I've never liked seeing that photo because Aida, despite her revived spirits, was physically drained, and I feigned a peaceful state that I didn't feel. I tried to look at the two of them with affection; however, my eyes barely hid my anguish.

[September 11]

45. Landscape dyed gray

I felt like a superior being, able for the first time to dedicate myself day and night to a cause, or more precisely to a person. I lived for the day-to-day, for Aida. I spent hours at her side, gave her the pain medications, answered the phone, took messages, prepared dinner, and took Mauricio to school. She would become distressed, and I lived her distress; she suffered, and I lived her suffering. I declined invitations to go out at night, even the ones from Paulo Marcos. I had gotten an informal leave from work. My boss liked Aida, understood that she needed me and didn't deduct a penny from my salary.

But if some god had accepted the offer I'd made at the Garden of Salvation, others had found it offensive. The metastasis spread. The doctors didn't recommend surgery or consider that Aida needed to be hospitalized. The medications were only palliatives.

On a December afternoon, we were admiring the blood-red royal poincianas bending over the hedgerow, with the cambuí trees in the distance, when Aida, altering her tone of voice, took on a grave expression:

– Tânia would be a perfect woman for you. She likes you, that's easy to see. She asked you to be her daughter's godfather . . .

– What are you saying?

– I'm going to die. You shouldn't be alone.

– No one will ever replace you, I declared, full of admiration for the grandeur of Aida's heart and for her magnanimous gesture.

I didn't deserve either Aida or Tânia. In reality, I didn't deserve women, always more loving and wise than I was.

[September 12]

In the only photo of Aida's last days her sallow, drawn face communicates an air of resignation. She's surrounded by her sisters, Mauricio in front, against the yellow bedroom wall. An aura developed over the course of her life illuminates the moral and spiritual dimension of her deteriorated, weak body.

At the funeral, only one person's presence displeased me; it was Stepladder, who barely knew Aida and came uninvited. He irritated me talking about his projects. A large beverage company had bought several of his photos for a publicity campaign to be exhibited in newspapers, magazines, on television and on billboards all over the country.

I didn't take photographs of the funeral, not even of Aida's body. Her image in the funeral casket, however, is engraved in my memory more than any other. There her goodness and her love for me were forever preserved. Surrounded by the perfume of flowers, her face was all her faces, including her youthful one, the one I had seen for the first time twenty years earlier. Death highlighted her love for others, her religious feelings, and her dignity. I was left with a wound that not even time would be able to heal. I had lost something irreparable, unique, and irreplaceable. The life remaining to me had lost its color.

I had no right to anything of hers. Nor did I want anything of hers, with the exception of Mauricio, if I could. I would keep only the silver heart engraved with our names.

I took photo # 45, the first one after Aida's death, on a cloudy afternoon following her funeral after those months of peaceful agony. I'd drunk my beer alone in the bar where we went often when I had the sudden realization that Brasília had changed in its most minute details. The entire universe had been dyed gray, as if a new copy of a technicolor movie had arrived in black and white. No other landscape could be more familiar. Nevertheless, the buildings, the interquadra posters, the signs full of numbers, the clover leaves of the little axis highway in the distance, everything seemed strange, beneath the even light of an overcast January.

46. Bigfoot and Termite

Around that time I moved to my studio at the end of North Wing and returned to the Ministry. Some of my co-workers who hadn't gone to the funeral gave me their condolences. Others threw me a distant look that I attributed to one of two reasons: a malicious comment by Violeta about me or simply having lost Aida, my godmother and protector. On my desk I found a letter from Livia sent some time earlier. She thanked me for the photographs but forbid me to publish them.

I called Mauricio from there. I felt responsible for him and wanted to fulfill my promise to Aida.

– Never call my son again, you bastard, Mauricio's father yelled from the other end of the line, interrupting our conversation. Pay attention to what I'm saying. Bastard! If you call again, I'll break your face, you creep.

The world had changed and so had the mood of my department manager. She announced without preliminaries that in a month's time she would no longer need my services.

I felt like a trapeze artist without a net, about to fall. Seeing my pirouettes in the air, Antonio would have the definitive proof that I should have listened to him: "Life also means working and building something." I had dedicated myself to life. Life before, life ahead of and above everything. I had lived for women and, at times like that, it was women I still needed most. But among the ones who had loved me, Eva had committed suicide and Aida had died. I imagined myself at a charity bazaar being auctioned in front of an audience of women, all the ones from my triangles seated like a uniform mass, and Joana standing large as life right before me. At the announcement of the auctioned object, in other words, me, they showed their bodies and an ironic smile. Not one would give a red cent for me. Joana would be the first to say I was worthless. Would Tânia, whom I could now clearly see in the first row sitting with her legs crossed looking at once serene and engaged, be willing to buy me for my sale price?

Only photography redeemed me; it's all I had left. If photography was a way of seeing the world, I had started to see it in a different way, and I owed that change mostly to Aida. Aida had been guided by higher values. Her memory helped me face life with less cynicism, and she would have been happy to know about my new photography projects. I should also admit that I wasn't indifferent to the criticism of my exhibition, which may have contributed to my being even more receptive to the suggestions that Aida had made when she was alive. Besides, I weighed in my considerations the fact that I was losing my job, and taking photos of the most squalid satellite cities could bring me some monetary return, as opposed to the photos I had been taking. Above all I was attracted to the idea of taking photographs of Vila Paulo Antonio. I was tired of Brasília's gigantic arches defying the smallness of man and the laws of gravity. I would compose a photographic essay about the contrast between the futurist city and the anti-Brasílias, between the modern monumentality and the open sewers, between the light, airy structures and the dirty walls rising from the ground.

The difficult thing was to create an original work, one that would bear my mark. I decided to visit Bigfoot in Papuda Prison. I had to see him; I shouldn't put off the meeting that would have to take place sooner or later. I wanted to acknowledge him and take his photograph. I wouldn't plagiarize Stepladder; my style was different, and they would be photos only of Bigfoot, not of any other prisoner.

I set foot in a prison for the first time. If Stepladder had come there and taken photographs of so many prisoners, why couldn't I visit my son and get authorization to take his photograph? I was prepared for the worst. I knew the jail's horrible reputation. Three prisoners had been killed in a prison rebellion less than a month earlier. Although it was visitors' day, I waited almost an hour. While I was in the lobby I met reporters interested in the story of the Mexican singer Gloria Trevi, who was incarcerated there in Papuda. She was accused of kidnapping, rape, and corruption of minors and according to reports had become pregnant after being raped by two prison employees. I didn't know yet how I was going to approach Bigfoot, and I didn't have the slightest idea what I would say to him.

– What's up? he asked me with an expression of displeasure. Because he had seen me with the reporters he thought I was one of them.

I noticed a mocking smile on his angular black face, where I sensed a mixture of suspicion and fearlessness. With large, alert eyes and short curly hair cut almost to the scalp, he was a tall, robust man who disguised his insecurity by developing muscles.

I was improvising what to say one word at a time. I introduced myself as a friend of Berenice and Ana, I knew Termite, I had arrived in Brasília several months ago, was a photographer . . . At first, I didn't dare ask him to pose for me, especially considering I wasn't allowed to enter with my camera. But I hinted at my interest in obtaining permission to take his photograph.

– To appear in the newspaper?

– No, no. Don't worry. I don't know what I'm going to do with the photographs yet.

– Then I'm not interested, buddy. Get lost.

What did Stepladder have that I didn't have? Why had he been able to persuade all the prisoners to pose for him and I couldn't convince Bigfoot?

– I'm going to spend some time in Vila Paulo Antonio taking photographs, I told him.

He seemed impatient, not understanding the reason for my presence.

– Berenice told me about your house in Vila Paulo Antonio . . . Would you consider . . . renting it to me?

The idea came to me naturally, and was also helped along by the need to pay cheap rent when I could no longer count on my Ministry salary. Ever since Aida's death I'd been going through a hard time, my life seemed without meaning, and I avoided going out even with friends . . . Why not live in Vila Paulo Antonio for a while like a monk in a spiritual retreat and on top of that be able to take whatever photographs I wanted, and perhaps even sell them?

– No good. I'll need the house real soon.

– It would only be for a week, two at the most.

– Depends on the money. I need some money. I wasn't able to snag a job in here, you know? They're reserved for the guys with good behavior. I'm what they call a "non-classified."

We came to terms on the rent, and I left there with the impression that I'd participated in a good business meeting. Business creates friendships, that's what I hoped.

Berenice called me, furious, when she heard directly from her son about my visit, and she tried to keep me from renting the house. Faced with my determination, she begged me to say nothing to Bigfoot about what transpired between us. She preferred it that way. That he never find out.

I set up my darkroom in Bigfoot's house, but I'd have to leave it in two weeks when he got out of prison. I completed a series of photos of landscapes that would have nurtured Aida's heartfelt rebellion; streets that had followed a plan inspired by Brasília and had become filled with disorder and poverty. I framed trash and sewage in spots as deserted as a crime scene, where sometimes an anonymous person wandered by. I wasn't robbed or assaulted, perhaps because of the respect that Bigfoot's house conferred in that Vila or for a simpler reason, the one that I'd once explained to Aida: nothing probable ever happened to me.

I quickly realized that those photographs were cold. Neither dreams nor imagination fit in them. Squalor isn't just an objective piece of data. It doesn't consist of precarious materials, or the nonexistence of things or food. It needs a face where the feeling of privation and unsatisfied desire can be seen. I wanted to take photographs not only of need but also of envy, desire, and revulsion.

I had already acquired the skill of photographing people—politicians and women, mainly. Now I would use my camera not to glorify people or to celebrate them or even to criticize them but instead to understand them. Following the precepts of great masters of photography, I snapped the camera's motor on a woman I came across by chance on the street as if it were a machine gun searching for the exact moment and the correct exposure not only of light, mass, and texture but also of poverty, exploitation, and dignity. In one of the photographs I took, a group of women is seen from the back. They're in line for the government's monthly food basket. Just one woman—the one I was photographing—looks back, in the direction of the camera. On her face wrinkled with indignation and despair, in the corners of her crinkled eyes and in her semi-open mouth revealing missing teeth, I read a protest against the behavior of the photographer, who was exploiting her squalor for aesthetic and commercial ends. Putting known theories into practice, I wanted to surprise her so that her shock would reveal some secret, some previously hidden quality or characteristic and capture her unconscious movements, which after the photograph would become the obvious, visible reality. Her protest was justified: I did in fact have the tendency to aestheticize squalor, and, in the end, the only reason the photograph turned out not to be a saleable product was because the editor of the local newspaper, whom Guga had introduced me to so that I could denounce Eduardo Kaufman, didn't want to purchase my photographic essays on Vila Paulo Antonio.

The result of that essay didn't satisfy me either. I ought to seek out the collaboration of the people I photographed, as Guga had suggested. My photos should reveal what was special and unique in each one of them; I should know their names and establish, if not a relationship, at least some contact with them. The solution would be to salvage my project of transforming Bigfoot himself into the main character of my photographs.

I had a brief conversation with him on the eve of his release from prison. I didn't want to act like a tourist or a hurried reporter, I told him. Could he be my "guide" or "teacher" in Vila Paulo Antonio?

– I'll pay another week's rent if I can continue using your house. I wouldn't even need to sleep there. I'd just leave the equipment there and use it as a base to continue the work I've started. It would be a matter of sharing the house with you for no more than one week.

I didn't tell him that it was also the way a father had found to help his son without his knowledge or that I wanted a chance to spend time with him so that we might forge a friendship.

– Okay. Termite gave me the dope on you, he answered to my surprise, agreeing to my proposal immediately. Later I learned that Termite had reciprocated the kind words I'd sometimes directed at him with praise for me. Through Termite's stories Bigfoot saw me as a famous photographer and also as a degenerate, which seemed like a virtue to him.

Our differences brought us together. I felt good being accepted by him. I admired his bold and rude temperament as well as his sincere words. He felt like a celebrity having a "famous" photographer dedicated to him, interested in his gestures and movements, which facilitated my main objective: earning his trust. During the first week, I photographed the joy of his reunion with friends. We drank at a bar near his house and then walked through the streets like bums with no destination. I took photographs of poverty's details while Bigfoot and his friends, Termite among them, smoked marijuana.

One week stretched into two, and during the second they let me photograph them in action. They guided me into the underworld of their underworld, to the drug dens and houses of prostitution, in short, to the reality that Aida so liked to quote. A reality with an inhuman face that I could portray with much more life and richness than Stepladder could.

– Today a stray bullet passed through a body during the funeral, Termite told me laughing.

That was soon a pretext for talking about famous crimes, growing violence and murdered friends. I thought it was better to cultivate that camaraderie than to reveal to Bigfoot the secret Berenice wanted to keep.

They were bums. No, bums are people who do nothing. They did things. I don't want to talk about drugs or police involvement.

So I'll limit myself to saying they were always busy with their mischief. To be frank, I was amused by it all, despite the headaches resulting from the mixture of worry and cheap cachaça.

My new photographs of Vila Paulo Antonio revealed its interiors, Bigfoot's friends, and daily activities. I saw myself as a photojournalist of newspaper columns.

One photo marked the moment at which I knew I had earned Bigfoot's trust. In the black and white photo above, taken in a Vila Paulo Antonio bar, one notices the contrast between the muscles of Bigfoot's large torso and the visible ribs of Termite's skinny body, between the look of defiance of the former and the sneering gaze of the latter with a cigarette hanging from the corner of his mouth. The idea was theirs, to have themselves photographed bare-chested with the billiards table in the background. I deliberately captured them in movement as if the photograph were announcing the future with gestures. I felt that not only had they accepted me; they liked me. They saw me as an unusual individual who was amused by their pranks. They didn't have the slightest concern that I might use the photograph against any of them.

[September 13]

47. Family portrait

Without the job and until I gathered a new clientele, it would be difficult to pay rent in the Pilot Plan. Family was good for something. I borrowed money from Antonio.

– If I can't pay off this debt, brother, you can deduct it from my share of the inheritance when Mother dies.

– You don't want to kill off the old lady before her time, he protested. And why don't you stay with me for a while?

I accepted, specifying that "a while" wouldn't go beyond Carnaval, or more precisely beyond the days required to find an apartment.

– You've lowered your standards, Cadu. Who ever heard of living in Vila Paulo Antonio?

– I wanted to take photographs . . .

– No excuses. It's dangerous. It's not even a place to visit.

I moved to Antonio's house, taking my photo equipment with me.

On the very first day at breakfast I was embarrassed when Veronica tried to make me into a model for Antonio:

– Look at your brother. He's almost the same age as you and he really looks a lot younger. He enjoys life, he has fun.

I denied it categorically:

– I don't like the life I lead, even less so now.

– But this is a phase, it'll pass quickly. Now in Antonio's case . . . He's really out of touch.

Antonio didn't answer. She'd always been this way. She was chatty and expansive; he taciturn and reserved.

– Marriage is a difficult art, brother. Veronica isn't perfect, but no one is. Besides, it's worth building something that lasts, a family, a legacy, leaving children well settled in life, Antonio commented privately to me.

– Your brother doesn't have the slightest sense of humor. He's rude, Veronica told me, when he left.

That night when she was ready to go to a party with him she complained that he hadn't noticed her outfit.

– There's no outfit that doesn't look great on your body, sweetheart, he answered.

– Don't start on me with your irony. And don't call me sweetheart.

– I notice your body first, the clothes are secondary. To be honest, I prefer you naked.

– Don't be a smartass!

– Why is it, Cadu, that women are always dissatisfied? Why is undivided attention too little? They want to spend the rest of their lives as the little girl everyone notices, "look how cute she is," "how charming," "what a pretty little dress," Antonio said.

Since he now refused to escort her to the party, Veronica declared categorically:

– Then I'll go with Cadu.

I would have never accepted that demand if it weren't for Antonio's own insistence. He made it clear I'd be doing him a big favor if I went with her.

While watching Veronica sway her hips gracefully in a tight dress, I stayed at the bar emptying one glass after another and thought of my brother's statement: "I notice your body first, the clothes are secondary . . ."

The photo above, # 47, was taken the next day: Antonio with his right arm around Veronica's shoulders and my nephews in front of them, all smiling in the garden of the North Lake house. I'd already noticed that Antonio and Veronica hadn't touched each other in a long time. No kisses, no caresses. I'd heard the harshest words from one about the other. That time, in response to one of Antonio's complaints, Veronica yelled at him:

– You're always reproaching me; you never pay me a compliment. If you don't like me the way I am, why are you married to me, you prick?

Antonio tried to give her a hug and a peck on the cheek.

– Don't come near me, she said, with a look of disgust.

The photo, taken at my niece's request, relaxed everyone's mood for a moment. It's a typical family photograph, similar perhaps to billions that exist worldwide, but this photo with its harmonious appearance is always the one that comes to mind when I think how unreal and false a photograph can be. A photograph of a lie. But no other reminds me better of those days spent in my brother's company. It's also the only one I ever took of Veronica, and, for reasons that I will yet explain, she deserves a photographic record in my book.

[September 14]

48. Tânia's belly

The following Sunday, Antonio invited Guga to lunch. To my surprise, Tânia, with her eight-month belly, came too.

The rain upset Veronica's plans to hold a barbecue outside.

– I hate this city, she said. I can't wait to get out of here.

– You only like a place after you leave, Antonio said.

– It's just that our life only gets worse. With each new phase I discover that it was better before.

– We already know hell is the present. The past and the future are always better, Guga agreed, and then he compared Veronica to the *Goofus Bird*:

– According to Borges, it's a bird that builds a nest in reverse and flies backwards. It doesn't care where it's going, only where it has been.

I noticed Tânia's enraptured look as she listened to him.

– Who's Borges? Veronica asked.

Later on, while I was busy making and drinking caipirinhas on a corner of the veranda, and the other guests were occupied with their plates, I asked Tânia about Paulo Marcos.

– I don't know where he is. He doesn't keep in touch. It was better that way, you know, Cadu? The relationship had stopped working. But forget about Paulo Marcos. Tell me what's been going on with you. You disappeared!

With the courage the liquor was giving me, I dared to ask:

– Are you seeing Guga?

– What an idea!

– Guga certainly wouldn't be the right person for you. He's untrustworthy. He's irresponsible.

– Look who's talking, right, Guga? she said.

– I turned around. Guga was behind me. He turned his back on us, and as he prepared to leave I added for his benefit:

– I know I'm not depressive and paranoid like he is.

I was happy to see Tânia's belly and to know that my goddaughter, who would seal our bonds of affection and friendship, was growing inside her. Tânia let me photograph her belly appearing as a perfect curve in a black dress with white polka-dots against the smooth peach background of the living room wall. A clear, simple photo, able to cleanse my thoughts.

September 16

While he was helping me locate the photo of a white ipê tree today, Mauricio confirmed that he's been going out with Laura for several weeks. My first impulse was to convince him to give it up. But perhaps because the resignation of the old had conquered the cruelty of the blind, deep down I was relieved and even pleased. Their relationship brought me back to reality. I'm no longer a teenager living on illusions, nor have I aged to the point of underestimating the beauty of young love. I add the happiness of the first to the happiness of the second and I'm twice as happy.

Mauricio wants to help me get back together with Guga.

– He's the one who broke it off.

– And if he came to see you?

– He'll never do that. He harbors his resentments for the rest of his life. He's not the type to forgive.

– But if he comes? Will you see him?

I changed the subject so that I wouldn't have to confess that I don't have the slightest desire to see Guga again.

September 23

I'm thinking about abandoning my Book of Emotions, *and not just because of the doubts I have regarding the pages I've written. The biggest problem is yet to come, because my old diary—the photo diary—ended a little after Aida's death. The only remaining serviceable photograph in the diary is the one of the white ipê Mauricio helped me locate. After the point at which my diary ends, I'll have to fabricate new thoughts and look through scattered files for photographs to go with them. Maybe this explains why I haven't written a single line this whole week.*

[September 23]

49. White ipê

I discovered one of Veronica's morning rituals after Antonio left for work. There was a play of reflections that began with the long mirror on the half-opened door of her bathroom. From a particular angle in the hall—or the entrance to the master bedroom—it was possible to see her in front of the bathroom cabinet as she was entering or leaving her bath. I had never felt attracted to Veronica. She hadn't even been my partner in the sport I'd invented on my dominical walks on the Main Axis, the game of drawing smiles from attractive women. Her thick lips and wide mouth were disproportionate to her short chin, and her nose turned up defiantly. Her front teeth were too large, and her semi-open mouth revealed too much of her gums. But reflected in the mirror as she undressed, her tall figure acquired an air of elegant vivacity. She moved her body to the music of the CD she left playing in her room, examined herself in the mirror from every angle with her slightly crossed eyes and ran her hands through her hair. She quickly removed her clothes and sandals. Above her buttocks she had two symmetrical dimples. To the left of where bikinis had outlined a miniscule triangle against the sun, dark marks were visible, probably a scar left from a wart. She had thin ankles and shapely legs. The breasts with their large areolae and erect nipples swayed with the movements of her body. She appeared distracted, staring vacantly and intermittently humming a tune. After getting out of the shower she examined her face at length and using finger pressure tried to undo her furrowed brow and crow's feet. After drying off, then firmly and unstintingly brushing her black hair, she slowly applied cream to her buttocks and thighs. I never tired of seeing her in the small variations of each of these routine movements and sometimes even used a pair of binoculars that I had retired when I left Rio.

One day, watching Veronica change clothes to go to the pool through the half-open bathroom door, I let her see me. She lingered naked in front of me as if thinking about what to do, definitely watching me out of the corner of her eye. I opened my fly and removed my hard dick, which I knew was impressive with its size. I imagined several possible scenarios: she running toward me and we ending up in bed; she covering her eyes with her hands, ashamed; I being thrown out of the house immediately, after being called a pervert, lecher, or exhibitionist; she laughing at me, politely considering me immature; she trying to cover herself, closing the door, and then telling Antonio everything.

None of this happened. She turned around, tried on a bikini, then another, let them drop to the floor, bent over to pick them up, and it seemed obvious to me that her behavior shouldn't be attributed to myopia; she wanted to show off her firm full ass deliberately and from the most varied angles.

I didn't like Veronica but over several days her slender nakedness insisted on appearing in the middle of the night in my grieving thoughts. I would fuck Veronica, I would fuck her in anger, and my anger liberated my lowest violent instincts. One moment I saw myself hitting her, throwing her to the ground, and the next minute my imagination had her kneeling, blowing me or on all fours while I buggered her. I was going to masturbate in the bathroom, thinking that one day my brother would catch us in bed, and not that he'd kill me for it but that I'd kill him in self-defense.

Two weeks later, and before any of my ruminations could come true, I was able to rent a small studio on the third floor of one of the interquadras in North Wing. The architecture of the interquadra was a dull pseudo-modern, departing from the original plan in which the exclusively commercial buildings weren't to be more than two stories high. The advantage was that now I could not only live there but also set up my darkroom.

Livia sent me an email. She was passing through Brasília and wanted to see me. I went with her to the Parkshopping Mall and afterward we had a salad at a South Lake restaurant. I had spent that month sleepwalking, not even noticing the city. The regular seasonal rains had spilled a fresh green on the grass and trees of the Main Axis. Several billboards carrying the photograph Stepladder had described to me at Aida's funeral advertised a beverage. I didn't envy the quality of his work, which as usual was low, but rather the amount of money for which an unscrupulous photographer sold himself to advertisers, which was surely high.

– I put all men in a drawer, Livia told me. Once in a while, I take one out. I use him a little and return him to the drawer. When I think the guy isn't worth the trouble anymore, I throw him in the trash.

I saw myself out of the drawer, ready for the trash. We didn't speak of our fleeting adventure or of Aida. We talked about the Ministry and what we'd been doing. We spent several hours together, perhaps hoping that some new chemistry would spark between us. But the ingredients of our temperaments were cooking in separate pots, unable to produce flavors of any kind, much less spicy ones. We said good-bye with cordial words and no promise to meet again.

A few weeks after my move, I found myself by chance with Paulo Marcos in an interquadra shop. He and Tânia had reconciled, he said, and she would give birth at any moment.

– I was about to call you. We wanted to ask you to be our daughter's godfather, he added.

I surmised that Tânia hadn't even told him about her earlier invitation to me. Although the surprise I showed was feigned, the joy with which I accepted the invitation for the second time was genuine. What a relief that Tânia had preferred her husband to Guga!

Time was being marked by the flowers, all recorded in my camera for my long-range project, my panel in honor of Brasília. I took photographs of the blooming white ipê behind my new building. I developed one of those photographs, # 49 (above), enlarged it into a four-by-three-foot chromogenic print, framed it, and hung it on my living room wall. I took it as a light, joyful symbol of a new beginning.

[September 24]

50. The fortune-teller

Carolina was born in the month of March and filled the emptiness Mauricio had left and that I would never have been able to fill, even with my own son. After having lived with Bigfoot, I realized that it was impossible to develop a satisfactory paternal relationship with a son who was so different from me, whom I hadn't seen grow up and whose upbringing I hadn't contributed to. I considered Carolina the daughter I'd never had. What a joy to be her godfather . . . When I visited, she recognized me, smiled at me, and came willingly into my arms. For days I had awakened smiling just at the thought she existed.

This joy went arm in arm with another, just exactly as Carolina went arm in arm with her mother. Deep down I was content with what I had, and I was rewarded with a nobility and peace of mind I'd never experienced before. It was enough to feel Tânia's fond look, the certainty that she liked me with a feeling coming from the bottom of her soul, to feel the outflow of her affection and dedicate my tenderness to her without losing Paulo Marcos's friendship or my respect for the love between the two of them.

[September 25]

The days passed in this habitual peace until one night after midnight as I was arriving home after drinking my usual cachaça at the interquadra bar, I was almost killed by two guys. They beat me up and threatened to kill me without saying why. I couldn't figure out a reason for the assault. I didn't have any enemies, they hadn't robbed me . . . I was seen at the emergency room of the Regional Hospital at North Wing, but I resorted to Ana's prestige to arrange a transfer to the Sara Kubitschek Hospital.

After reflecting on it a great deal, I came to the conclusion that no one other than Eduardo Kaufman could have been behind that attack. He was running for Congress and we were approaching the elections. My denunciations might not only have reached his ears but could also have begun to have some effect. Perhaps fearing what was still to come and above all the damage I could do to his campaign, he had ordered me killed: nothing less.

At first I considered my conclusion mere supposition. But I deduced that there was an extremely high probability that the supposition was true when I had a visit from Eduardo Kaufman and learned directly from him that he had been the intermediary of my hospital transfer. What could justify such kindness other than the need to throw me off the scent of his criminal act?

When I was absolutely sure Eduardo was the guilty one, there was only one question remaining: how to get even with him. Using the same methods? If I were in the Northeast or the Amazon, it would only cost two hundred reais to hire a hit man—and that was worth more than Eduardo Kaufman, who wasn't worth anything. As a matter of fact, to say that he wasn't worth anything was to overvalue him. In truth, he made a negative contribution to the world; his value was less than zero.

Fortuitous circumstances delivered an answer. One day Bigfoot and Termite came to see me in the hospital. They were shocked by my cast and the bruises from the blows I'd received. That unexpected visit brought us back together. So much so that when I felt better I returned to Vila Paulo Antonio to continue my photo-essay.

On a Saturday afternoon after walking through the streets of that satellite city in search of new faces or angles, Bigfoot brought me some top-quality marijuana and the two of us joined in harmony with the universe, sharing our intimacies and ignorance. This is how I found out about Bigfoot's aptitude for robberies and lightning kidnappings, while he learned of my hatred for Eduardo Kaufman.

– Virtue isn't worth it, Bigfoot said.

He was making plans to get together enough money to move to the Lake.

– I want to eat high-class pussy, he announced.

My plans were more modest: to take revenge on Eduardo Kaufman. I had not only the key to the universe but also to his apartment. I discarded my plan to be an exemplary guide for my son. He was a grown man, I wouldn't be able to change him. He was the one who could perfect me, freeing in me a certain dose of malevolence to be directed to the right person. We combined my hatred with his greed and began to plot the strategy for my revenge.

Bigfoot proposed staking out Eduardo's arrival in order to kidnap him. He wanted money, a lot of money. I, on the other hand, thought it'd be better to act in the absence of Eduardo, who was at that point focused on the final months of his election campaign. I only wanted his computers, all three of them, on which I would find the proof I was seeking. I didn't want any money, much less to become involved in a kidnapping. I was too cowardly for that.

– Nothing but the computers, I repeated.

Deep down, I was a good person. The good are afraid, they never know for sure and that's why they leave room for doubt. They're not able to close their eyes or cover their ears. On the other hand, the bad are sure of what they do. They're passionate and they don't weigh the consequences of their actions. Maybe they do weigh them and have the courage to face death without fear. That was Bigfoot.

It was already dark when I left his house. On a nearby street a fortune-teller's sign caught my attention. At the window a woman with large eyes invited me inside. She took me into a darkened room with rough whitewashed walls, on which a crucifix could be seen, and laid the tarot cards on the table.

–Who's the tall dark woman smiling at you? she asked, showing one of the cards.

Since I didn't answer, she added:

– She's going to appear when you least expect it.

It couldn't be Tânia, she had fair skin and I was always waiting for her. I remembered Antonieta and what the medium at the

Garden of Salvation had said, that there are no missed appointments or accidents, only fate dictated by the wisdom of time.

The fortune-teller also foresaw the outcome of an old dispute:

– A satisfactory solution will require a great deal of daring on your part.

Although I didn't believe in fortune-tellers, it made sense to be my most daring in the case of Eduardo Kaufman which, on second thought, meant agreeing with Bigfoot. Bigfoot could do whatever he wanted to as long as he brought me the computers. Let Eduardo get his just deserts, equal to the assault on me. I didn't need to tell anyone I had his computers in my possession. I would simply extract additional information from them to incriminate Eduardo and, based on this, I would supply the newspapers with solid leads.

I thanked the fortune-teller for having opened the doors to my future. As I left I took the photograph above, # 50. The window frames her gentle figure in blue. She has very large eyes trying to leap out of her round face, wavy hair down to her waist, and a body out of a Botero painting. In the foreground, to the right, a *pequi* tree displays its exuberant blossoms in five hairy brushes shaped liked yellow fans. In the left corner the moon is an enormous illuminated biscuit rising at the end of the long avenue lined with small trees and light posts.

[September 25, night]

51. Ballet with police van

I didn't need to go to Vila Paulo Antonio to take the photos that Aida had so often suggested. The next day, a Sunday, near the bus terminal several police officers kicked two blacks into a police van. The men reacted by kicking back. They were then held down and had their arms twisted. One of the officers started beating them with his nightstick.

– It's a lie, I didn't do anything! said one of the beating victims.

– Shut up, shit-head! yelled an officer.

People began to gather. I, who always avoided crowds and fled scenes of violence, was enjoying being there calmly witnessing the events unfolding. I wasn't afraid to take a bullet. There was something heroic in my attitude. If I were to die it would be like dying for Aida. I was prepared to accompany her to the next world.

– You have to respect human rights, a girl screamed.

– To hell with human rights, yelled a middle-aged man. Hooligans deserve beating.

– Let them go, they didn't do anything, shouted a street kid.

Images forced themselves in front of my camera. I would take photographs of the feeling of impotence in the face of injustice. One of the prisoners managed to get free. An officer fired into the air. A confused ballet enveloped me, people leaping in all directions. I was the only one who continued watching the scene at close range. I snapped the lens on the last scenes until the prisoners were placed inside the police van.

I printed one of those photographs. It's a shame Aida was no longer there to see it. If I were to write about it, I would talk about the crowd's protest and the use of the expression "human rights." Maybe it was for good reason that no one was on the side of the police, just as rarely was someone on the government's side, be it left, right, center, or sprawled in all directions like a compass rose.

What had the boys done? Certainly the treatment used on them was proportionate to the amount of African blood they carried in their veins. Perhaps they had broken some law, but there were laws and there were laws, the ones enforced and those that weren't. Aida would have said, correctly, that if I followed those prisoners and unraveled their stories I would surely discover moving dramas, endless anguish, great tragedies—and that was reality, something much larger than my skepticism, cynicism, or indifference.

If I had any doubts about the social or pedagogical function of that photograph, it seemed less doubtful that it would earn me a few reais. It was a good photojournalist image that I should sell to a newspaper. I added it to the ones I had taken in Vila Paulo Antonio. It's # 51 (above).

[September 26]

52. Akiko on an August afternoon

No matter how much I disbelieved the fortune-teller's words, I couldn't forget them. I was determined to employ all my daring against Eduardo Kaufman and I hadn't expended my ammunition yet. While waiting for the computers Bigfoot would bring, I could execute my Akiko plan. I didn't have money to squander on prostitutes, but Eduardo Kaufman justified my extravagant investment. It would be the first time I'd bonked anyone since Aida died, ending a seven-month abstinence. Akiko plied her services in house calls, in hotels—as long as the client paid the bill—or else she saw clients in an apartment not far from mine in North Wing, which I preferred. I paid the extra twenty percent for full service, interested in what she could tell me.

Not only had she heard of Eduardo, she even intended to vote for him in October if she could get to São Paulo, where her voter's registration was filed.

– He's handsome and a great speaker, she said.

– Have you gone to any of the parties he's given?

– What parties?

– You're covering for him.

– Are you here to talk or what? she asked, lying on the bed.

She opened up for me in every possible way, but no matter how much I tried I couldn't get a hard-on. She sucked me, slowly massaging my testicles gently. She caressed my anus with her slender fingers and with her tongue, promising that it would definitely excite me, and nothing. She sucked me again, applying her best techniques. When the delay began to seem a losing battle, she said:

– You're a hopeless case. The first guy who couldn't get it up with me.

I tried several more times, rubbing my penis against the entrance to her vagina, her buttocks, thighs, breasts, lips—nothing doing. Eduardo Kaufman was getting in the way of my erection. Akiko was unrelenting. She wouldn't deduct the twenty per cent surcharge.

– In a case like yours, I should charge a lot more.

I didn't place the blame for my failure on the fortune-teller. Perhaps her prediction hadn't been wrong; it was my daring that had been insufficient.

In the end, I proposed to Akiko that I substitute a photograph for a fuck. She agreed if I'd pay her double. Standing naked in front of the computer monitor chewing her nails, she reminded me of Marcela. From her Asian heritage she'd retained not only slanted eyes but also a gentleness of movement and tenderness of speech. I set up the camera and took photograph # 52 (above). The arrangement of the space and the books on the shelves are those of an educated woman. Her slender, lithe body and small bottom have almost no tan lines. Her body is tattooed with a red and black bird below her navel and is totally waxed between her thighs, where the vertical line of her sex is clearly and discreetly visible. Akiko leans her head to one side like a bird. Her look has something angelic about it. Her jutting lower lip is like a baby's, about to cry.

Thus I diligently began to classify my failures, which I called experience, so that they serve as a step stool for the final, fatal blow to Eduardo Kaufman.

53. The strategy of appearances

I recall it was September of 2002, eight months after Aida's death, and I was alone with Tânia in the living room of her apartment. Carolina, seven months old, was playing in her pen.

– Enjoy it, I told Tânia. This is the golden phase of babies. They know how to sit but they can't run yet.

Tânia was silent and pensive. We stood at the window close to each other, looking at the mango trees and also the bougainvilleas that seemed to want to bloom early.

– I'm still taking photographs for my panel of flowers that I'll soon consider completed.

Those bougainvilleas brought back the memory of some royal poincianas, or, more specifically, a conversation I'd had with Aida.

– Aida told me I should marry you.

– And you, what did you think of the suggestion?

– You know I've always liked you.

– There's Paulo Marcos . . .

– Will you put me in line, then?

– You're not just first in line. You're the only one. She gave me a maternal kiss on the forehead.

– And Guga?

– It's crazy for you to be jealous of your brother. It's offensive even. Don't forget I'm a married woman.

She spoke in a serious tone but soon emended it with a smile:

– Silly . . . She pinched my cheek and ran her hands through my hair as if wanting to muss it.

Ever since my conversation with Tânia at Antonio's house Guga had stopped talking to me.

I held Tânia's hands.

– Agree to have dinner with me?

– What am I going to tell Paulo Marcos?

– Isn't he away?

– I'd better not. I'd go out with anyone else but you.

– May I know why?

– I'd rather not say.

I tried to kiss her.

– Stop. I said you'd get your chance. But you have to wait your turn, and behave yourself.

– All right, if you tell me you love me.

– I love you.

We kissed slowly.

– Ah, she sighed. That was the last one. From now on our agreement applies. Promise?

That kiss unleashed exaggerated confessions on my part that I'd been in love with her ever since the first time I'd seen her, and on hers that she'd had a hot dream about me in which "everything" had happened. We kissed again.

– If Paulo Marcos weren't such a wonderful guy I could do something crazy, she finished.

I don't like the photos I took of the mango trees that early afternoon. They're too trite, as trite as the mango trees in Brasília. But photo # 53 (above), with its colors striped by the bougainvillea shadows against the noonday sun taken on the same occasion, could never be trite for me because it's inextricably linked to that kiss.

54. Failure achieved with great effort

I only heard about the robbery at Eduardo's apartment when the police approached me. Bigfoot was such a moron, a simple theft of electronic appliances! Since no door to the apartment had been broken down, I was suspected. Bigfoot hadn't been in touch, not even about the computers.

I didn't turn him in to the police even when they decided to arrest me. I spent only a few hours in jail. Eduardo Kaufman had me released and then called:

– I know you're innocent. You could never do something like this.

[October 5, night]

I looked for Bigfoot.

– I need to tell you something very serious, I announced after several draft beers at the bar.

– If you want to get any money out of this business, forget it. There were no computers there.

– I'm your father.
– What's this? Have you gone nuts?
I told him all the details.
– You're my father? He shook his head, seeming not to believe it.
– I want a photo with you.
– No. Forget it. He turned around, perhaps suspecting I wanted to hand him over to the police.
– I have so many pictures of you, I said, to remind him that I didn't need anymore if that were the reason. But I don't have one of the two of us.

He still refused to pose. That's the reason for photo # 54, from the back, white letters printed on his tight red T-shirt, a yellow cap with red embroidery in the shape of a Chinese ideogram worn backwards in the direction of the camera, loose wide Bermudas over strong stocky legs, cell phone hanging from his belt like a pistol, multicolored lights on the left side. A photo the photographer wanted to throw in the trash but the father kept. I had failed, and that was the photograph of my failure, another for my collection. A failure achieved by great dedication and effort.

October 7
After so many years, two days ago Bigfoot came to see me, which led me to recall a photo in which he appears from the back and that my goddaughter Carolina helped me locate yesterday. I then inserted it in my Book of Emotions.
Today he's a respectable fellow with at least one great dream fulfilled: he lives in South Lake. I noticed from the hug I gave him that his body is even bulkier. While he was talking I could hear the light tinkling sounds of several bracelets on his restless arms. He decided

to file a lawsuit to force me to acknowledge paternity and he's demanding a DNA test. *He may think I'll be leaving an inheritance and doesn't realize my debts total more than my assets, even if he got a good deal for my Hasselblad and my old Leicas.*

– The test isn't necessary, *I told him. Recognizing you as my son, as far as I know the only one I have, is fulfilling for me. It will serve as proof of the greater meaning of a passing pleasure.*

Nonetheless he wants the test.

October 8

Carolina reminds me more and more of her mother, even in the attention she pays to me. She wanted to come have lunch here and brought me food she'd made herself: pork loin and stuffing. We talked about the fantastic developments in genetics and medicine, the challenges of the Amazon and the Northeast, the continual poverty, the most recent wars, and the world's new economic geography. I'm old enough to know that the future we glimpsed never was and never will be attained, but I'm still young enough to live without past or future and most of all to talk leisurely with a charming young woman.

– When reality disappoints, don't give up. And never stop enjoying the good side of life, *I advised her.*

My goddaughter offered to help with the organization of the photos if Laura can't come as often. The possibility startled me.

– Why can't Laura come anymore?

– I'm not saying she can't, I don't know. She didn't say anything to me. *I just think that having to reconcile her work with the duties of a housewife . . .*

– But she can keep working in my darkroom. The darkroom is hers.
I prefer not to know if Laura and Mauricio are about to get mar-
ried. It would be a mistake for them to make this kind of decision
in haste.

[October 10]

55. Lost photo or the logic of chance

In the years following Aida's death I slowly became a guy with few friends. Alone, I drank to forget her and some days I drank to the point of getting drunk. Once in a while I agreed to spend Sundays with Antonio and Veronica as long as Guga wasn't going to be there. Veronica smothered me with attention. Our relationship seemed like one of former lovers. It was as if we knew each other's secrets. Her nudity had softened the anger I'd felt for her. In this way, I forgave her more easily for everything, even and principally for existing.

In late October of 2002, I participated in the parties for the presidential election with her. Days later, in November, I selected with her help a group of photos of Eduardo Kaufman in ridiculous and comic poses alongside Paulo Antonio or Ana. Eduardo had been elected congressman from São Paulo with the highest turnout in the country, carrying on his coattails four more of his party's candidates who had barely received any votes. The photographs that Veronica and I selected could at least cause him some political damage.

My collaboration with Veronica had not only the consequences for my future that I intend to discuss later but also, in the present, led me to think about the dark-skinned girl the fortune-teller had seen in the cards. That girl remained in my thoughts for entire days with Veronica's face. Then she showed a prettier face than Veronica's and gave me a spontaneous smile that had never belonged to her. Little by little she grew even taller and her body became even darker and more exuberant than Veronica's. Wasn't it Antonieta I'd been thinking about in the fortune-teller's house?

I saw her rarely and always by chance. I got up the courage to contact her. The pretext was to give her as a gift one of the photos I'd taken in the Water Hole Park, the one of the Japanese landscape, that here was given the number 10. The gesture that I'd imagined serving as the start of a new relationship dissipated right there. She received me with polite coldness and didn't notice the emotional charge stored in that photograph. On the other hand, I was added to her email address list and thus I received her forwarded messages and, after she married, also news of the birth of each child accompanied by photos. Over time I understood I'd wanted to win her affection not out of love but out of vanity. Besides, women are flowers that should be picked when they first bloom. Once the moment is past they can wilt. Nevertheless, my memories of Antonieta brought me joy because in the memories the flower was newly blooming, ready to be picked.

I've said I became a guy with few friends. But reducing those "few" to their essentials, I had in truth become a guy with only two friends. In fact, Sundays in the company of my goddaughter alleviated my loneliness, marking the weeks, months, and years. I bought her gifts, pushed her stroller on walks in the park . . . In this way I kept my friendship with Tânia and Paulo Marcos, who frequently invited me over.

At their insistence, one night—it must have been in 2004—I accompanied them to the opening of Stepladder's art show. I knew of his success. His name always came up because of the prices he charged for his photographs that were now printed on plates, cups, and design objects. He had become an entrepreneur of his artwork. I never saw him except at some bar, always in the company of Paulo Marcos.

Chance has its mysterious ways. That night I ran into Marcela who was thrilled to see me again.

Over the next few days I went to one of the Sunday lunches at Ana's house and Marcela agreed to accompany me. They were lunches always awash in copious amounts of alcohol at which Berenice continued to avoid me, even though I had promised not to contact Bigfoot anymore.

I saw Guga there for the next to the last time. They were discussing politics, and I'd come to the conclusion that mutual affection and common opinion didn't always go hand in hand. I could agree with everything Guga was saying despite our strained relationship. And I liked Tânia more and more, although I disagreed with her political romanticism. She was such a passionate defender of Paulo Antonio that she even felt admiration for everything Eduardo Kaufman had done to resurrect the former President's memory. I felt like a Muslim who wanted to marry an Orthodox Jew, or a Huguenot who had fallen in love with a Catholic during the religious wars.

From local politics they moved to the Middle East and the Iraq War.

– They use principles and morality to suit their purposes. They're arrogant and they shamelessly lie. One minute they're in favor of dictatorships, the next they're supporting democracies, said Guga.

They all clearly condemned the use of lies and disrespect for international law, except Paulo Marcos.

– Everything depends on the direction of world events, on the possibility for democracy in the Middle East . . . In politics, what matters is the outcome.

– Are you one of those who believe that the ends justify the means? Guga asked.

– Are you talking about here or the Middle East? Ana wanted to know.

– It's been said that freedom has to be earned. Who ever heard of forcing anyone to be free? Carlos declared.

– There can be actions that are morally right but politically wrong. Just as there can be politically responsible acts that are morally questionable, defended Paulo Marcos.

– You should do what's right, come what may, Tânia said.

– According to the ethic of conviction. Now, according to the one of responsibility . . . Paulo Marcos continued.

– And the ethic of irresponsibility? That's the one for those who close their eyes to what's wrong out of selfishness, loyalty to a cause, obedience, or simply because they think that's the way things are, Carlos ventured. A kind of ethic of complacency.

– Paulo Marcos and I always have this disagreement, Tânia said.

– Well, I don't know about here, but over there the culture's different. It should be respected. If they don't want democracy . . . If it's the women themselves who want to live that life . . . Marcela volunteered.

– Let's talk facts: the world isn't rational; rights get tossed into the trashcan when they conflict with interests, and everyone uses their own power. But I don't agree with your relativist position, Marcela. Some things should be defended anywhere, Guga said.

– In matters of culture, nothing is definitive. Even the worst cultural conflicts can be undone over the long haul. Look at my case: I'm named for one of the New Testament apostles, I'm the son of a Jewess and married to the granddaughter of Syrian Muslims, said Paulo Marcos.

Ana pulled me into a corner to complain that I'd sold her photographs to Eduardo Kaufman.

– Those photographs are pretty tame. They're the same ones I gave you.

– And you think that makes it all right! she said indignantly.

Even now, I think her reaction was the result of Eduardo's perfidy. He probably blackmailed her with those photographs, exaggerated what they showed, or related the circumstances of the sale in such a way as to disparage me in her eyes.

At the end of the afternoon I took Marcela to my studio. I still hadn't broken the habit of counting the minutes. After one hour and one whiskey Marcela and I were in bed. At the end of two it had been easier and less enjoyable than I'd imagined. Sex with no guilt or consequences; also with no pain or pleasure. Supermodern and superbanal.

Marcela was the first woman I'd taken to bed with any success since Aida's death, already more than two years before. But that night of sex made me especially miss Joana, whom I hadn't thought of in a long time. Only she and no other woman could have broken that back and forth between desire without sex and sex without desire. I was going to send her an email or, better yet, a letter by regular mail. I fell asleep an obsessed idealist: I wanted to get back what I had lost, the one I had lost.

I awoke a realist. Joana was unobtainable. She hadn't been in touch ever since she'd returned to Rio. She might even be seeing Eduardo Kaufman. She'd probably become one of his lovers.

Marcela was there beside me, available. I kissed her breasts. That was enough to set her on fire like one sets fire to paper drenched in alcohol. The youth and lightness of that skinny girl had their advantages: Joana wouldn't have been able to do pirouettes or bob up and down as much on top of me; she wouldn't have had the same excited little ass when she made love. We traded the most crude and vulgar exchanges, I used the foulest profanities I knew and yelled whatever else I could to shock her. Marcela wasn't to be outdone. She dominated that rich vocabulary better than I did and she wasn't intimidated, as if she'd had experience with phone sex. She talked fast and a lot, like noise or static from a radio that's never turned off, but even so I turned it off in order to concentrate only on her figure and her movements. She was still naked in bed displaying well-trimmed pubic hairs, two narrow strips in a V between her legs. She groomed them like someone who grooms a moustache. Her body was a good match for her spirit: fine, distinguished and courteous. She was skinny all over without a millimeter of fat, muscle right against the bone, exact thighs. She might not have given me the generous and succulent pleasure of a Joana, but she had made me happy with her happiness, and I still liked her name: Marcela.

– If I have a daughter one day, I'll give her your name: Marcela.

This made her even happier, and with her increased happiness she made me even happier still, irrefutable proof that happiness is a highly contagious virus. As a matter of fact I liked her name and I repeated, as if it were now a prophecy, that in order to complete my destiny on earth I would one day have a daughter named Marcela.

– I already have a son.

– You never told me.

– He's a criminal, a burglar. I think even a murderer.

She laughed, thinking it was a joke.

– Did you know a fortune-teller foresaw that a brown-skinned woman would suddenly appear in my life?

Her full breasts were rigid with perfect curves and round, dark, erect nipples.

– They're beautiful—I felt them.

– You're not the first to say so.

– If I were going to remake my panels project I would do it with breasts. Circles instead of triangles. There are an enormous variety of sizes, colors, and shapes. And if we add the shapes, colors, and textures of the nipples . . . I agree with the theory that nature can be entirely represented by triangles, rectangles, and circles.

Good-humored, she agreed with me and described my hypothetical panels with rich details as if she had composed them herself.

When I set up my camera she fled from my field of vision like a skittish cat. That explains the lost photograph (# 55) in which only an unmade bed and Marcela's right hand appear, blurred in the left corner. If her panties and the condom I'd used were lying on the bed, I'd claim it was a photograph in the manner of Tracey

Emin, the British artist who transformed her bed into a work of art. But what would be the value of a photo of an empty, unmade bed, rumpled sheets, and pillows thrown to one side?

The value would be considerable, I don't hesitate to say; the value of a faithful, steady companion for a man who suffered the bitterness of his solitude. The proof is that I kept it for years on end. That photograph was like a note to myself, a kind of scribble that shouldn't be shown and that I appreciated secretly whenever I wanted to evoke a pleasant night with no strings attached.

October 10, late afternoon
Laura asked me today (rightly so) if I don't have other photographs of Marcela. It doesn't seem correct to abandon certain characters in the middle of the story, but what can we do when they disappear in real life? Could it be that just because she wasn't the great love of my life or because she no longer kept in touch, Marcela didn't deserve my writing? Perhaps in the revision I'd substitute the stories of the skinny girl with just one sentence: this is my bitch Marcela, whose name pays homage to a former . . . Friend? Fuck? No, girlfriend! "Girlfriend" was the term she used in her conversation with Laura.

Now that Laura is about to be married, our friendship is even closer. I lost my fear of telling her about myself to the extent that this afternoon for the first time, while we were listening to music, I was able to verbalize the place in my life occupied by Joana and the mothers of Mauricio and Carolina. The love story that I narrated to her in short chapters is different from the one I've written in my Book of Emotions. *It emerged spontaneously. While I was talking, I became clear about what seemed confusing earlier, and Joana was present from start to finish. In reality, I think and I hope that my story with her hasn't ended.*

– I told her about you. She feels affection for you, Laura said. Don't you want to write to her?

The last time I saw her was seven years and forty days ago in circumstances that I should relate in my book. My life was made of small failures and missed opportunities, a life lived inside out, not for what I was able to accomplish but for what I didn't achieve. Joana exists to prove my thesis and to bring me the memory of what could have been.

[October 11]

56. The last flowers

I was happy to donate my photographs of the satellite cities, including the ones I took with Bigfoot in Vila Paulo Antonio, to a philanthropic entity interested in retrieving and organizing them, having placed one on the cover of its brochure.

I was even happier when I got a good price through an agent for the collection of photographs I had selected with Veronica, the ones in which Eduardo Kaufman appeared in comical positions alongside Paulo Antonio and Ana. A buyer who didn't want to be identified acquired the whole collection at once. In politics yesterday's enemies can be today's friends, but every politician has enemies in the present. Therefore, I surmised that some enemy of Eduardo could make excellent use of those photographs. Time had reduced my pretensions. Since I hadn't been able to wreak major revenge, minor revenge would satisfy me. No, I did not nor would I ever forgive Eduardo.

I would be lying if I said I was successful in what I was doing, but I had been able to survive without great difficulties. Then I began having problems with my vision. Maybe someone in a situation like mine would take the opportunity to recount a long tragedy. I prefer to be brief and limit myself to saying that, although it has been a shock knowing there is no cure for this disease, my anger didn't last long. My frustrations fit neatly into this paragraph. Little by little I was becoming resigned to my new condition, like someone who forms calluses in order to walk on coals. I lost my lateral vision at first and, although I was medicated as soon as I detected the disease, I was only able to slow the speed of its progress. I reached the point that in the viewfinders of my cameras I saw blurry figures, colors more than shapes, shadows . . . Anyone looking at my photographs saw the clarity and the sharpness that I couldn't see and that if I had seen I might not have photographed.

My vision problems were a radical watershed in my life and my photography. I changed my habits. I was obliged to take systematic rests. Out of necessity I developed the virtue of patience. The disease saved me from bad books and slowly withdrew me from the superficial, hectic world of images into the world of reflection. Thus I began to listen openly to the echoes of my own thoughts.

The photo *par excellence* of that watershed was taken in November of 2005. I remember it well because there was "something rotten in the state of Denmark," with Commissions of Parliamentary Inquiry investigating fake or rigged bidding practices, padded bills, unlawful use of pension funds, illegal payments, slush funds for electoral campaign financing . . . and Eduardo Kaufman hadn't even been cited.

The photograph captures the blood-red royal poincianas bent over the hedge with the green and yellow *cambuí* trees in the background. Against that same background one day Aida had talked to me about Tânia. For the first time, I noticed that my eyes no longer saw with perfect sharpness, and I didn't know yet that those were the symptoms of the cruel disease. It was the last of the photographs for my panel of flowers, # 56 (above).

[October 15]

57. Reality is also flowers

Because of my growing vision problem, in general I earned less money from the recent photographs than from the older ones, especially the ones in my archive of Paulo Antonio Fernandes to which Eduardo indirectly contributed as the principal promoter of the rehabilitation of the former President's memory. Paulo Antonio Fernandes was being discussed in films, TV programs, and books. His name filled squares, streets, highways, and airports.

But one day Tânia bought the panel of flowers as a gift for Paulo Marcos. I'd been composing it for years; it included photo # 53 with the bougainvilleas and concluded with the flamboyant. Of all my recent works it was the only one that sold for a good price, I suspect due to Tânia's charity.

It was as if without realizing it I were composing that panel exclusively for her. That day, I had a dream about Tânia: she was lying prone on the bed, and I was gently removing her flesh-colored panties and noticing that there were pimples on her buttocks. She turned over and tried to cover herself with her hands. Her breasts rose. Her protruding nipples, like aroused penises, pointed forward.

"I don't need anything else. This is enough. I'm happy knowing you want me," she was saying. I saw with perfect clarity, and all the colors were bright, so bright they gave off heat. In the dream Tânia had pinkish skin and a fuller body than in the original. She looked tall. Her thighs were long, her buttocks well shaped and arched. I just didn't understand why she had those pimples.

I never saw the flower panel assembled. I gave precise instructions to a framer on the positioning of each photograph in the panel, in which the rainy season with a green background contrasts with the dry season in a pale yellow hue. The photograph of the whole set, shown above, was taken by Tânia herself.

[October 17]

58. Marcela jumping on me

As my blindness progressed, I had more time for leisure. I learned Braille to occupy myself with reading when I'd lost my sight completely and one day, sixteen years ago, around April of 2006, I acquired Marcela to accompany me on my walks. The federal attorney general had denounced forty politicians and businessmen for racketeering, and I wanted to know if Eduardo Kaufman was among them. I could no longer read and had to ask a neighbor for help.

It was frustrating to confirm that Eduardo had escaped once again. On the other hand, my neighbor's bitch had had a litter and two of the puppies were for sale. When one of the female pups started jumping on me, the name "Marcela" came to mind. I had promised Marcela I'd give her name to my daughter. The three-month-old puppy hanging onto my legs was the closest to a daughter I'd had or would ever have, and I still found the name beautiful. I did a test. I called her: "Marcela!" She came running into my arms. I had fulfilled my promise. With no daughters or cats, I would name my dog Marcela.

[October 19]
Carolina, then four years old, pulled Marcela's tail or ears while Tânia and I speculated about whether Rio or São Paulo was more violent now that the mafia war by the Prime Command of the Capital dominated the São Paulo scene, and whether Eduardo Kaufman was included among the leeches, the parliamentarians who, by amendment, extracted money from the national budget to purchase overpriced ambulances for municipal governments.

– No. He's too rich to need to do that, she asserted.

– I heard on the radio that scientists measured the distance between Brasília and hell. It's only forty kilometers.

Then we all went downstairs—Marcela, Carolina, Tânia, and I—to stroll around the block. Seeing her poorly outlined and using the automatic shutter, I took a photo of Marcela jumping on me. She laughs and looks askance, as if she were a person. I would be exaggerating if I said I was happy, because happiness is a mirage we can see when we look backward or forward. But nothing was making me unhappy, and having my faithful companion Marcela kept me closer to happiness.

October 19, night
A few years ago life in the Pilot Plan was still peaceful. Today the swelling of the surrounding communities asphyxiates the city.

203

Millions of people fight over the scarce water and limited urban space. And I imagine that it's because of the kilometers and kilometers of asphalt that it has hardly rained at all, the air stays dry and the weather hasn't cooled off. The heat is intolerable today.

Mauricio and Laura came by and solemnly asked me to be best man. I accepted willingly. They seem made for each other. They prove that marriage is far from being a bankrupt institution. I've just been unlucky.

They asked Joana to be the maid of honor.

– What do you think? Mauricio wanted to know.

– I don't think anything. It's not my marriage. And if she accepted . . .

– She was really thrilled when we said we were going to ask you to be best man.

I had also never been so pleased and not because I think Joana's interested in me. Maybe it's because of the wedding atmosphere, because I'm surrounded by young love and see Mauricio and Laura happy.

[October 22]

59. The mechanical eye

Time was marked by the varying degrees of my vision loss and my corresponding inability to take photographs, until a few years later I reached the phase of photographs of darkness, photographs of voices and other sounds, sometimes mere noise or what touch and smell revealed. When my weak sight unsaw things, my memory and conscience revived them. I saw what my eyes couldn't see. The colors of our surroundings only exist for our eyes, which capture almost nothing of the world's light. But when our eyes go dark those colors cease to distract us and our eyes feel free to explore what is beyond mere appearance. Over time I grew convinced that truth can be clearer in the dark of the blackest night, and I discerned another meaning for the sentence Guga had uttered and which I had never forgotten: "Man's eye serves as a photograph of the invisible, just as the ear serves as an echo for silence."

Since my photographs of voices and other sounds weren't marketable, I stopped working. I was being supported by Antonio with my future money, in other words, I finally persuaded him to agree to deduct his cash advances from my inheritance. When my grandfather died, Mother had preferred to move from the ranch to Porto Alegre where Guga was living. With the sale of the land she'd acquired a nice house, an eighth of which would one day be mine and would be combined with my small self-employment pension to pay for my food deliveries.

My inheritance didn't take long to arrive. I didn't want to ask Antonio for money to go to Mother's funeral nor did he offer any. So my financial debt to him didn't increase, as opposed to my debt of gratitude to her. I'm not a man to cry even when there's plenty of reason to, especially since as a child I cried for no reason. But when Antonio told me Mother had said my name in a coma just a few hours before she died, I cried my silent heartfelt cry. Her absence loomed larger than I could have ever foreseen. I dreamed about her several times. I know how much she loved me and how little I knew how to return her love. I rarely paid her a visit. We spoke little, besides the exchange of banalities by phone.

Antonio also told me that those had been her exact words a few days before: "Tell Cadu to contact Guga. I want them to reconcile." In the depth of my stubbornness I always followed her teachings.

However I ought to discard that advice. Guga was the one who had stopped contacting me. And why had Mother not directed the advice to him, the one who had arrived in time to witness her death?

Once in a while I drank more than I should, thinking about Mother and also still thinking of Aida. I could no longer see enough to walk alone outdoors. One day as I staggered home I was struck by a car. Thrown against the sidewalk, my head hit the curb. I shouted at the driver. Still holding the camera that I insisted on keeping with me, counting on my luck not to be robbed, I tried in vain to take a photograph of what I couldn't see, the car that was leaving without giving assistance.

– He's crazy, a boy yelled. Others around me laughed.

I made out the deep voice of a teen:

– Leave Cadu alone.

Once again the improbable had happened to me: my camera remained in one piece and it recorded some scenes in response to the nervous movements of my index finger. They tell me that in the blurry photograph reproduced above (# 59, which proves the hypothesis of an *optical unconscious*), the light is mysterious, there's a colored movement in the shape of an "s" and the plasticity of a work of art. A mechanical photo, whose framing was set by the camera's objective eye, an eye that sometimes surprises by seeing more than the human eye and that was able to record for all time not only that exact moment but also what came later.

[October 22, late at night]

60. Touching Tânia

The voice I had recognized was Mauricio's. He wanted to take me to the hospital. I refused. I had felt only some slight dizziness and the injuries appeared to be superficial. He finally left me in my studio and dressed my wounds. Later I had a call from Tânia. She was on her way. Mauricio had let her know.

Since I still refused to go to the hospital, Tânia insisted on redoing the dressings, perhaps to confirm that the accident wasn't too serious. She wanted to know if the fall had been hard, if I felt head pains. Paulo Marcos had traveled to Miami on business, she said.

That night I had a nightmare. I dreamed I was embracing Tânia; I'd discovered that I truly loved her as I had never loved another woman. She was hugging me and she said we'd be happy. We were holding hands leaving the bedroom and when we opened the door we ran right into a wall. "The door is further ahead," Tânia said. We walked a few more steps. When we opened the second door we saw Paulo Marcos accompanied by Mother. He had an angry look on his face and Mother had a surprised expression, not yet knowing how to react. Then she accused me with a harsh look: "You committed a grammatical error!" I awoke with a start, feeling that Mother was sitting there beside me on the bed.

Tânia and I went out together several times. When I was with her, her interest in what I was saying made me feel intelligent. Words came easily, quickly filling the too brief time for everything we had to say to each other. I didn't always agree with her. She had hard-line political positions and believed in the leaders of her party, especially when they were the opposition. But I forgave her political opinions as much as she forgave my indifference. There was only one thing I would never forgive, and for this reason I never asked her what had happened between her and Guga because I didn't want to hear an unacceptable answer. I also never learned whether she told Paulo Marcos about our meetings.

I spent years fantasizing about the day he would die. I didn't wish for it exactly. I liked him. But when I placed on one side of the scale the lightness of the sincere friendship I felt for him and on the other the consistency and solidity of my feelings for her, the scale tipped toward the pan with the affection, admiration, and desire where my love for Tânia lay. Tânia's complexion was not dark but she could get a very dark suntan, her eyes and hair were black and seeing her again had been unexpected. I didn't even need to believe in the tarot cards to bring the fortune-teller's prediction to fruition. I thought several times about reminding Tânia of our earlier conversation and telling her that when she was free I would be ready for us to live together.

With time, I finally understood Guga's earlier lecture about desire and happiness. He was right, desire had made me suffer, because we want what we don't have, and desire is like a cell that reproduces itself easily. As soon as one is satisfied another appears. I was able to free myself from my desires, seeing the world in a disinterested manner and, despite the advance of my blindness, acquiring a peace I had never known before. It was good not to be able to look at myself in the mirror, to cease admiring the shapes of my face and lamenting the visible signs of aging, as if Narcissus had finally been convinced by the blind Tiresias that he'd live better if he didn't see his reflection. Perhaps I was less focused on myself. Being happy in Tânia's happiness was sufficient.

I serenely contemplated the world that had so tormented me. It now idled impassively before me, like a shining, seductive, fancy dress forgotten on the bedroom floor on Ash Wednesday morning after keeping me awake on Carnaval night. I came to value the ascetic behavior of someone who wants to accomplish something greater than himself and to build virtue through resignation. It was possible to fight against vanity and renounce material aspirations. I just couldn't forgive Eduardo Kaufman.

One day Tânia and Paulo Marcos took me to a concert in the Martins Pena Theater. I left Marcela at home and went out with my cane. The odor of the old velvet, carpet, and cleaning products made me queasy, when to make matters worse Eduardo Kaufman came over to talk to me during the intermission.

– I wanted to tell you that I was the one who bought the photographs you took of me. They're really funny. I've shown them to friends and they're a big hit. If you still have any more, I'll buy them.

His words unleashed the anger I had been saving for years. I needed to at least punch him. It was an act of desperation, my settling of old scores, since I hadn't been able to do anything else and never would. I located him with my cane, clenched my fists and shot my right arm in his direction with all my strength. The strike at the air threw me off balance, almost knocking me over.

– Are you crazy? he said, avoiding me as I tried again and again.

Finally, with all the violence I could muster, I struck a blow to the outside corner of the wall. Thus my revenge was summed up in an attempted blow and the only noticeable result was my bloodied hand.

Tânia witnessed it all. She was understanding and—I believe this is the right word—loving. Having her faithful friendship, life seemed to roll by like a lighthearted movie, a daydream that allowed a beam of reality to shine—a reality that didn't delude and couldn't disappoint. When she came to comfort me the next day I asked her to pose for me. I touched her hair with my fingers to be sure of the framing of her face, and her lips to measure the expression of her smile. If they told me she was no longer beautiful, I wouldn't believe it because my touch confirmed the image my eyes had preserved intact. Photography stops time and can retain feelings so that they can be relived in memory. The photo above (# 60) was the last I took of Tânia.

October 30
I asked Carolina for news of her parents. She gave me their email addresses.
– They'd love to hear from you.
I sent a brief message to Tânia, saying that my goddaughter had been keeping me company and that Brasília was never the same after she and Paulo Marcos left for Miami.

November 2
It's been nine or ten days since I wrote a line for my Book of Emotions. *I wasn't feeling well and I believe that's why I thought about settling scores, now that I'm better: to pay homage and express my gratitude to the deceased. Following my suggestion, today Carolina, Mauricio, Laura, and I went to the cemetery.*
It had been some time since I'd ridden across the city by car. I went with my goddaughter. We took the Main Axis, and I was measuring distances according to the number of cloverleaves that I recognized by the loud hoarse noises of the car tires. With each curve and stop, I went on guessing the places we passed.
Knowing Brasília isn't about knowing the Esplanade of the Ministries or the Plaza of the Three Powers or the superquadras, or even

South Lake or the satellite cities. Inside me I felt the weight of its drama, intrigues, contrasts, its chaos disguised in straight lines, its worm-eaten dirty modernity, its dust, light, hot sun, the rot of the power dungeons, the spilled tears and laughs heard in the corridors of Congress, so many actors, my memory of desire, an essence of the desert, of nothingness, everything from which I plucked my remnants of hope. I saw myself as a fool who wanted to recover Brasília's myth and utopia, its beauty and dream of equality.

The quantity of flowers we carried revealed the number of our dead. First, Mauricio and I deposited flowers at the foot of Aida's grave near the stone with the phrase "I fought for justice and lived to make others happy." I asked Mauricio to clean and restore the words that Aida's sisters had had engraved. It's a simple grave as are all the graves in Brasília's cemetery. I covered myself in the shadow of the trees growing around it, inebriated by the smells of the wreaths we had brought. In front of Aida's grave, I kissed the silver heart she gave me. I like rituals.

I asked them to take me to the graves of some friends I never forget and who are also there under the ground. I don't believe in life after death, but it's as if in some way they were still alive for me. As if through those flowers we'd brought I could communicate to them how much of what I am—mainly whatever good there is in me—I owe to each of them. I kept smelling the flowers we were passing and tried to identify the perfume of each one.

We found Carlos at Ana's grave, where the smell of jasmine was strongest. He asked me about Guga.

– I have no idea what he's doing or where he is, I answered.

Carlos may not know about my battles with Guga. He saw us together at Ana's funeral a few months ago where my brother and I *didn't say a word to each other, although he came over and hugged my shoulder as if to say "let's forget the past" or perhaps "we should cry over our common past together."*

Ana's greatness hovered over Carlos and me. I became emotional at his emotion, expressed in his voice. Unfortunately, Ana died before we had the chance to renew our old friendship. She was more offended than I could have ever imagined over such a small thing as the sale of her beautiful pictures to her ex-husband and lost confidence in me. Carlos never learned the real reason why Ana put distance between us and continues to be kind to me when we meet.

He invited all of us to go to his house. These days I recognize houses by their smells and, on arrival, the smell of that house reminded me of the previous times I'd been there. It was as if Ana's spirit were making itself present in the smell given off by the furniture, rugs, and wooden beams.

– It's a shame they've never allowed public access to the lakeshore, Carlos said, and described the landscape, speckled with so many sailboats.

I added his description to the old photo I'd taken from that same angle and that way I saw perhaps even more richness of detail than anyone else present.

We remained on the terrace talking about our deceased for the better part of the afternoon and in that regard Carlos recited a Portuguese poet:

– "Death is mute. When death speaks, it's because it's life."

Judging by the length of our conversation, Ana's death was a life that would never be extinguished.

I asked about Berenice. She was bedridden. They took me to her room, which reeked of mildew and urine.

– I don't want you getting involved with my son, she said when they left us alone. Her voice showed her fragility and advanced age.

I attributed the comment to her senility. I wasn't involved with Bigfoot and I wanted to be honest with her and myself:

– He's my son too.

– No, no he's not. I should have told you a long time ago. It was my foolishness back then. He's not your son. Listen to me. Please forgive me. It's all my fault. All mine, she repeated. It was my lie. I was all mixed up back then. I needed money. Forgive me. I don't want to die with this weighing on my conscience. I don't, I don't.

She seemed lucid and sincere. I was disconcerted.

– You're making this up.

– Why would I make it up?

– So I wouldn't contact Bigfoot.

– I know he's the one who contacted you. I told him the truth and he didn't believe me.

I have the impression that the driving forces of my life were pure winds, but strong winds, the kind that give meaning to movement and sweep up anything lying in their path. I'm still mulling over the sentence: "He's not your son." Now it makes perfect sense to agree to Bigfoot's request: I'll take the DNA test. For me, he was always the proof of Joana's infertility. If I don't submit to a fertility test as well, it's only because I'm too old for that now.

Now I can be the true blind Brasiliarian—and with all the beauty to which I'm entitled—in that story of Clarice's, which I decided to listen to again:

"Brasília . . . was inhabited by extremely tall, blond men and women who were neither Americans nor Swedes and that sparkled in the sun. They were all blind . . . The more beautiful the Brasiliarians

the more blind . . . and the fewer children they had. The Brasiliarians lived around three hundred years."

I lack only one quality: to be able to live three hundred years.

61. The visible and the invisible

I tried in vain to forget Eduardo Kaufman. He was popular and had been elected to a third term. He was in the news as a member of the Ethics Committee and a promoter of new bills to reform campaign financing and combat corruption, thus helping nurture a national taste for long-postponed bills that, once passed, would never be enforced. As if this weren't enough to invade my day-to-day life, one day he sent an aide to see me.

– The congressman knows how you're feeling and the difficulties you're facing. That's why he insists on helping you.

Eduardo proposed to collect the photos I had taken of him into a book, and he'd pay me for my permission to show them.

I thought hard about what to answer. It would be the second time I'd sold myself to him. Besides that, his purchase of those photographs had been totally out of line. How many reais were my principles worth?

I concluded that I wouldn't be selling myself. Eduardo didn't realize the trap he was falling into. The revenge I'd planned kept diminishing in size with time, but on the other hand it was becoming more viable. This plot was miniscule but it was concrete and possible. I gave the authorization he requested in writing and in exchange he sent me the payment for the corresponding amount. The price of each photograph was low when compared to my earlier photographs of Paulo Antonio. Because there were so many of them, however, the amount was sufficient to cover the monotony of my routine for several weeks.

The grotesqueness of those photographs wasn't an invention of the photographer's eye. It was manifest in the subject's movements and behavior. Could there be any better proof than the theatrical photograph (# 61, above) in which Eduardo Kaufman appears with his mouth open in the pose of an opera singer with half-closed eyes alongside a stupefied Ana? The ad for a well-known bank, visible in the background, is an allusion to his crooked dealings. The money bills and the slogan that—due to the framing of the picture—was limited to the word "contribute" refer to the illicit funds that circulated in his campaigns. The small child going by who appears at the bottom in the foreground, a poor Indian with a distended belly, as well as the word "never" prominently visible on the poster hanging behind Eduardo, add another suggestive layer of interpretation. I chose that photograph for the cover of the proposed book given the clarity of all of its planes, its luminosity, and its excellent color contrast.

November 2

Almost midnight on November 2, after so many years of not using my camera, I now took a series of photos. Only to me will they not be mysterious and incomprehensible. They're of keys and two wedding bands atop a rectangular piece of black lace placed in a box, recalling a work by Joseph Cornell. I felt like a naughty boy. I cut up the lace from Joana's panties that I had kept for so many years.

Lewd thoughts don't ask permission to enter one's mind. If I try to push them away, they become more present. If I insist on hiding them under the name of modesty and common sense, they get aggressive, like a bull attacking me, like African bees threatening to kill me, like a dog barking at me nonstop.

November 3

They barked all night. The once young man saw himself again in Joana's room in Rio, she rearranging her garters and parading from one side to the other. I remembered that Carnaval I spent with her in Rio, listening to the clamor in the streets and to what she was saying, that no fall of a government would measure up to the memory of our meeting. Paulo Antonio and all of his era are worth less than Joana's perfume, embraces, and moans on that distant afternoon. Could I still hold her in my arms even if it only meant that our skin would touch? I wonder whether she's still fascinated by Eduardo Kaufman.

November 8

I've fallen ill and so I haven't written for several days. Yesterday Mauricio came to visit me.

– Is it true that you intend to dedicate your book to Joana? he asked, adding that she's already in Brasília.

– First, I haven't finished it yet. Second, I don't intend to publish it. And third, I have written mainly in memory of Aida. I don't like sentimentality or objects, but I never got rid of the little silver heart that Aida gave me and I grow sad when I think about her.

I was mixing half-sincerity with good manners. I say that I was half sincere, not because I lied but because I omitted the rest. I should have confessed that if Joana came in here today, I would trade everything I've written for her embrace.

– Why don't you publish it on the Internet? It would be read even more and would still earn you royalties.

Mauricio dialed a number and wanted me to invite Joana to visit me.

– No, not in this condition.

I'm suspicious that he or Laura has been reading my diary. They know too much about me. They even guess what I'm thinking. Whom I'm thinking about. I don't want to contact Joana. I'm afraid both that she doesn't and that she does want to see me. In the first case, the confirmation that she doesn't desire me will still cause me pain. In the second, I wouldn't feel any better because I'd see in it the promise of love, which at our age is mainly the promise of shared sorrows.

November 20

If the names of pain are many, as I came to write in this diary, then many more are those of pleasure. A few words, and mainly three exclamation points, were suddenly able to change my mood. Repeatedly, I hear the words of an email in the voice of the computer as if it were music. I will fully reproduce them here:

Dear Cadu,

What a lovely surprise to receive your email. Paulo Marcos and I are well. Miami is pleasant at this time of year. It's not as hot now. Beautiful days, blue sky, after the hurricane season that this year saw us almost lose the house. Paulo Marcos loves it here. I've adjusted now, even to the

American habit of periodically electing an enemy of the moment. Politicians have the power to simplify the world and to make everyone believe in a new map and new weapons.

And you? How are you? Sometimes we get news of you from Carolina. I'll never forget our many conversations. In our living room we have your panel of flowers, and it's with great affection that I keep the photos you took of me. I hope to visit you on a future trip to Brasília.

We received an invitation to Mauricio's wedding. Unfortunately we won't be able to attend.

Send news whenever you can. All the best from Paulo Marcos.

Miss you lots!!!

Tânia

I feel pleasure again in listening to the night music with its crickets, toads, and the roar of cars passing on the Main Axis, even the noise of the elevator and the neighbor's television; in savoring the taste of whatever touches my lips, in exploring shapes with my hands, in reading Braille, in smelling rain, the perfume of women, and even the stink of Marcela's coat.

I feel pleasure especially in learning of Mauricio's joy. Tomorrow will be his wedding to Laura.

November 22

Last night Carolina took me to the wedding in Don Bosco Sanctuary at 702 South. Churches have a particular smell. Perhaps it's the mixture of incense, candles, and flowers, not to mention the sweat of the crowd.

The sound of the violins reverberated around the walls. Laura's musical selection mixed something from Bach to the Beatles to Gershwin, besides some recent hits I'm not familar with.

Joana was there. I don't know whose idea it was to have me sit beside her. She was wearing one of her perfumes from the old days. She came over to talk to me and asked if she could visit me.

Guga gave me a hug, this time less timid than the one at Ana's funeral. I still have a hard time speaking to him. There will always be an open wound in our relationship. I felt we agreed on the basics: we're imperfect and for this reason incapable of erasing our resentments; but we forgave each other.

As I was leaving I also ran into Antonieta. The last time I'd seen her, many years ago, I'd noticed that time had passed for her. Her aging had been slowly approaching mine but then had overtaken it at great speed. Her eyes were sunken. They seemed faded and opaque. She'd lost her sensuality; her face was etched by day-to-day concerns and certainly by the years dedicated to her children.

It was my good fortune, therefore, not to be able to see her this time. Thus, I could imagine her young, in a Rio bar which then blended with the paths, sky, and lake of the Water Hole Park. She was accompanied by her husband and children, four in total, the oldest apparently a friend of Carolina's.

[November 22, with revision on December 9]

62. Physical love

Despite the aide's promises, months went by without my photographs of Eduardo being exhibited. There was also no news about the book. I who had initially hesitated to sell those photos began to await impatiently for them to appear. I called and complained. The aide explained that the project had had to be postponed.

One day, finally, with Eduardo already finishing his third term, the photographs were exhibited. In the interviews I did, I spoke sincerely about what I thought of him. If I said he was corrupt without proof, I could be sued. I revealed, however, that he had wanted to kill me, and I pointed out that his character was evident in those photos. They thought it was funny—even Eduardo thought it was funny—that a blind man could describe a photograph in its smallest details.

That was my only successful exhibit, and not just because being a blind photographer was a field day for the newspapers or because the public felt sorry for me. Eduardo was famous, and I had discovered pearls in his earlier life and had placed him alongside Paulo Antonio and beauties like the young Ana Kaufman. There was also the Stepladder effect, which elevated me several steps. At the opening reception, he put his hands on my shoulders, walked around the room a little with me and said:

– Pretend you're talking to me and we're close friends.

Photographs of our fake conversation later appeared all over the papers, together with praise from Stepladder himself about my work.

When it was finally displayed, I thought that the collection of photographs of Eduardo Kaufman could demonstrate a thesis about the photographed subject, his character and his flaws. On the contrary: to the commentators it demonstrated a thesis about the photographer, especially about my qualities as a creative humorist who had managed to magically transform a serious person into a grotesque one, a photocaricaturist who didn't resort to montages or manipulations. I felt like a child whose pranks adults thought entertaining. The photos were enlarged, reduced, republished in newspapers and magazines, reframed to highlight some detail or other and juxtaposed with "serious" photographs of Eduardo Kaufman taken by other photographers. I had done everything to fell Eduardo, but like that punching bag from my childhood, Bozo the Clown, he had teetered from one side to the other and in the end always bounced back upright.

I was misunderstood and, thus, recognized for the wrong reasons. They liked what I hadn't set out to do. What pleasure could I get from achieving glory by mistake? All that required my sensitivity, technical prowess, and intelligence would be buried and forgotten with me, if it didn't go into the trash first.

The repercussion of the exhibition was such that Veronica and Antonio, who were then living in Natal, learned about it on television. They called me from there. Veronica felt as if she were part of the project.

– I selected the photographs with you, she made a point of reminding me.

– You finally found your path, Antonio said.

For me, personally, the greatest success of the exhibition was that it attracted Joana's presence. I didn't expect her. She didn't stay at the opening reception long, but it was enough time to unnerve me. I wanted all of the other guests to depart and leave me alone with her. I needed to talk to her, to find out if she still felt anything for me. In the midst of the crowd, she greeted me effusively and left her perfume on my hands, which I didn't wash for several days.

Later she sent me a message reiterating her congratulations. I tried to call her several times and wrote to her, with no answer.

Because for me that exhibit became associated principally with her presence and absence, and also so that Eduardo's face doesn't appear again printed in this book, I prefer to change the photograph that opens this section. In the place of a photo from that misunderstood series goes one from the work destined for oblivion. The portrait above, # 62, is obviously of Joana. It was taken when I met her. I carried it in my wallet for a long time. It became wrinkled and acquired spots and the patina of time. One day, when I wanted to reproduce it, I preferred to make a copy from the print I carried in my pocket and that had its own story, instead of reverting to the negative. I digitized it and made a new print. The portrait was still there, subtler than in the original and with paler colors, juxtaposed with the hues that time and chance had applied to it. Photography can reproduce a singular instant for eternity and provoke the return of things forgotten, hidden, or dead. Joana's body is damp from the river water near Pirenópolis where we had bathed. Her dripping hair hangs down to her shoulders. She looks at me and there is desire and love in her eyes, a seductive seriousness in the shape of her lips. This is the photograph par excellence of that desire, the love I can't forget. A photograph that brings back the perfume and the softness of Joana's skin; that revives dormant feelings and has the ability through memory to resuscitate physical, carnal love in all its freshness.

November 30
Marcela has fallen ill. I suspect that she doesn't want to be left alone and for this reason she is racing me to the grave. Carolina offered to take her to the vet, if necessary.

I'm no longer so sure that I'm the handsome Brasiliarian of Clarice's stories, which I listened to again. "Brasília is the ghost of an old blind man with a cane going tap-tap-tap. And without a dog, poor man," she also wrote.

         December 1, night, in the hospital
Joana was leaning her body over my bed, supporting her arms on the mattress and the bed was starting to shake. Distressed, and no matter how much I opened my eyes, I couldn't see what was happening. Joana moaned and her body swayed. Now I clearly heard a man moaning right behind her, unleashing brusque, back and forth movements, Joana's skirt raised, brushing my legs. "Fuck me, Eduardo, fuck me," she said. "I want to give it to you. I want you to fuck me in front of this little shit." My bed shook even more. Besides not being able to see, a cloth covered my mouth and they tied me to the bed. Joana yelled louder: "Come, Eduardo. Come. Deeper, honey, put it all in." I tried in vain to free myself.
   I awoke in a cold sweat, feeling a deep uneasiness. The dream, all too real, affected me physically. My body is still sore all over, inside and out. My head weighs heavily.
   – You called the name Joana several times, and asked for your laptop, said a nurse who made my bed and tried to cheer me up with talk about a soap opera.

                    December 5
I felt a tremor when Tânia's voice approached the door of the room. The calendar receded twenty years. It was as if I saw her with the body and face from the time when I'd returned to Brasí-

lia. Without moving in the bed, I heard whispering between her and the nurse who takes care of me. We haven't met in five years. I almost asked her not to come in; memory was preferable to facing the present misery. But reality is the present and it imposed itself relentlessly.

I retrieved all the vestiges of my youth and put on a happy face. Tânia entered and sat on the edge of my bed. I knew that her face was serene and sad. The nurse, noticing the gravity of her expression, left us alone. For some minutes, Tânia left her hand forgotten atop one of my legs and we didn't say a word. Two hearts that had failed to connect were all that remained of our promises of love.

– I won't escape this one, I told her.

– You'll get better and be out of bed in no time. You'll bury all of us yet, Tânia told me with her protective maternal voice, holding my hands.

We were still alone and could say whatever we wanted. We wanted little. She brought me up to date on the news about Paulo Marcos and people we knew in common, not without revealing a nervous affection in her voice. I responded with farewells to her and the world without any regret, convinced that with all accounts settled, my life was a net gain.

– Get those ideas out of your head, she said. Tomorrow I'll be back.

– You're leaving already?

– I promise I'll come tomorrow and the day after. And every day as long as I'm in Brasília.

My goddaughter came in.

– Keep him company. And don't let him dwell on these morbid thoughts, Tânia told her.

– *There are more visitors coming, Godfather,* Carolina announced. I heard Laura's and Joana's voices.

– *It's just the way he likes it, always surrounded by female admirers,* Joana commented, in a cheerful tone. *Look how loved you are, Cadu. Your women are faithful.*

– *How are you feeling?* Laura clasped my hands tightly and gave me a kiss on the forehead.

– *Much better, now. Better all the time,* I answered.

Their voices were the background music that soothed me and, perhaps because they mixed with the effects of the medications, they ended up putting me to sleep.

When I awoke I was alone with Joana. I grew accustomed to examining the darkness in the back of my retina. In general, small stars float over a gray sea or I see orange circles, light bluish layers, dark brown rectangles on a light brown background . . . It was late afternoon and as I lay on my hospital bed I felt goose bumps. The color of death wasn't black, or gray, or purple, it was the color of sand bathed by a red sun that I saw with my blind eyes from the top of a dune. At the back of my retina, imposing itself on the customary blotches, Joana's form took shape. Colors blended muddily and I saw Joana undressing. It wasn't a dream. She was naked and young. A mound rose from my body creating pressure against the sheet. Joana revived me. I would trade my entire past for my little remaining future.

– *Come here, Joana, come here!* It was really her.

– *Cadu, honey. How are you feeling?* It didn't bother me to hear that question again because her husky voice caressed me.

– *Come here!* I tried to pull her by the thighs.

– *Don't exert yourself. You need to rest.*

– *Joana, have you come back to me? Have you come to share what little time I have left?*

– *I'm your friend, always.* And after a pause: *You don't deserve what's happening to you.*

Joana's perfume entered through my nostrils, mixing with the smell of ether in the hospital. I tried to grope her.

– *Calm down, I've already told you. Don't exert yourself.*

With the tips of my fingers I managed to touch her knees, which quickly pulled away from me.

– *Just tell me: would you consider coming back to live with me?* I insisted.

– *Don't make me regret coming.*

– *You're still seeing that bastard Eduardo Kaufman, aren't you?*

– *What a stupid question!*

– *Look on the closet top for a box I put together a few days ago.*

She's never stopped wearing high heels, whose clickety-clacks I heard move in the direction of the closet.

– *Those are the keys to your apartment,* I told her.

– *And why did you keep these keys?*

– *I don't know. It must be because I wanted to return.*

– *They wouldn't work. I changed the locks several times.*

– *See what else is in there.*

I heard her laugh. I felt the pleasure of someone who was rewarded for a lifetime of disciplined, persistent work.

– *And you, you never remarried?* I asked.

– *No, never.*

– *I want you to know one thing: you are the woman of my life.* Joana, I love you. I said the words with difficulty, they sounded like *clichéd sentimentality. When you love someone you don't have to say it, but I should. That desire to have sex with her I had never felt with such intensity for any other woman. I decided to call that intensity love.*

– You loved any skirt that happened by just as much.

– No other woman is like you. I truly love only you. And I don't put this in the past.

– You're not convincing, Cadu. You never loved me. Yes, I loved you a lot, but you never returned my love. One day I grew tired.

– It's never too late.

– If you could see me, you'd give up. I'm old and ugly.

– You're the same woman as ever. You have the voice, the eyes, the smell, the skin, and the body you had when I met you.

– Only the eyes, but not as bright.

– Tell me something: what is Operation Amazonia?

– Operation what?

– Listen to this sentence I recorded on my laptop. The hospital was silent while I located it. "If there is any crime that humanity hasn't committed yet, this new crime will be unveiled here. And so unsecret, so well suited to the plateau, that no one will ever know." It was another passage of one of those stories by Clarice.

– Mauricio told me you wrote a book for me.

– His imagination. I meant to write, but . . .

– You gave up?

– The book was to seduce you.

– I promise to read it.

– Then I'll give it to you the way it is, unfinished. The end will depend on you.

I'll skip the crying because I prefer the joy that followed it and that I could sense from the way Joana clasped my hands as she left.

– Before I die, I'd like to have one of your hugs, a full body hug. I'd like you to lie here on top of me.

– Don't worry. You're not going to die so soon.

The book will be for her, a more-than-open book, wide open, in which I show my whole self, with the hope that she'll take me back, even if it's only in thought. But in order for the book to be for her and no one else, I'll need to rewrite it. By persistently reworking the style, I can find a way to please her, to demonstrate all that she means to me and to eliminate the discrepancy between the love story I told Laura one day and what I've written up to now. I won't stop being faithful to who I am, however. In fact, I couldn't, because I carry with me everything I've seen and lived, everything I was unable to see or live, and I can't avoid taking on the features of all that I've lived over time.

December 7, six months and one day since
I started writing this diary

I dreamed that Joana arrived at my funeral and something awkward and embarrassing occurred. I had been buried with a hard dick. People snickered, and the fact was commented here and there. Only Joana cried. I tried to move, to get up to hug her. I had been transformed into a statue displayed in a public square, my granite penis pointed upward. Passersby laughed. I also felt like laughing, and seeing Joana's tears increased my desire to laugh. I wanted to laugh out loud, but my voice didn't come out, and my lips in the shape of a burst of laughter wouldn't move. Between the boredom and the suffering there were an orgasm and a laugh both sculpted in stone.

Then Joana was hugging me. Her wet body was as malleable as rubber, molded around the stone, and the stone that was merely a shell of my own body began to break apart. Joana hugged me more, and my skin became hypersensitive. I felt her embraces in my naked body as if for the first time.

I woke with the sensation that I won't die so soon. When I get to one hundred, medical science will take me to two hundred and from there to three hundred. I will thus develop another quality of the Brasiliarians from Clarice's story: I can live to three hundred years. The other characteristics I already have: I have no children, I'm blind, tall and, despite all the white hairs, I'm still blond.

If I could, I would photograph the end of that dream and print it on the walls of my mind.

December 8

No, it's not necessary to take a photograph of that dream. The photo already exists. When I look for something that might give meaning to life, I think about a distant summer Sunday when I heard the noise of the water, looked at Joana, so beautiful, and that mere look gathered everything around me, touching me in a profound way. At that instant my ardent skin inflamed Joana, and the pieces of the chaos fit together perfectly, giving meaning to the universe. I kissed Joana's wet lips and felt a shiver of tenderness and desire. My heart was a dream of futures among embraces and stars.

Every photograph is proof of a meeting, sometimes planned, other times fortuitous. It's a haiku stripped of rhetoric that captures only what is in front of the camera. It's no more than an instrument, an invisible window through which we see the object of our emotion. I have a photograph of that instant which could well substitute for #62. More than passing through time, it's time that repeatedly passes through it, successively revealing new details, new meanings for an expression, a look, or a gesture of Joana's.

Meaning is conferred by love and also by its absence; by that instant and by the distance that separates me from it; by the joyful moments, the shared laughter, a stroll holding hands along the seaside, and the doubts, the never-ending search, the nostalgia, the missed encounters, and even the incomprehension. My portrait is made up of the fragments of this scattered material. No single body is like any other, and Joana's has left its indelible writing in me for all time.

Without the instant, time doesn't exist, and without eternity the instant would be disfigured; it would cease being itself and would not be able to display always its unique, exclusive side. Photography has the ability to outlast its perishable materials as it reproduces itself, aspiring to eternity. I have the sense that when the world comes to an end its photographic images will survive.

December 9

I printed The Book of Emotions *to deliver to Joana. I made no changes except for the substitution of the last photograph and the addition of the final paragraph.*

JOÃO ALMINO is the acclaimed author of *The Five Seasons of Love*. He has taught at Berkeley, Stanford, the University of Chicago, the Autonomous National University of Mexico, and the University of Brasília.

ELIZABETH JACKSON is Visiting Assistant Professor of Portuguese at Wesleyan University. She is the translator of João Almino's *The Five Seasons of Love*, as well as co-translator of Patricia Galvão's 1933 novel *Industrial Park*.

SELECTED DALKEY ARCHIVE PAPERBACKS

PETROS ABATZOGLOU, *What Does Mrs. Freeman Want?*
MICHAL AJVAZ, *The Golden Age.*
  The Other City.
PIERRE ALBERT-BIROT, *Grabinoulor.*
YUZ ALESHKOVSKY, *Kangaroo.*
FELIPE ALFAU, *Chromos.*
  Locos.
JOÃO ALMINO, *The Book of Emotions.*
IVAN ÂNGELO, *The Celebration.*
  The Tower of Glass.
DAVID ANTIN, *Talking.*
ANTÓNIO LOBO ANTUNES,
  Knowledge of Hell.
  The Splendor of Portugal.
ALAIN ARIAS-MISSON, *Theatre of Incest.*
IFTIKHAR ARIF AND WAQAS KHWAJA, EDS.,
  Modern Poetry of Pakistan.
JOHN ASHBERY AND JAMES SCHUYLER,
  A Nest of Ninnies.
ROBERT ASHLEY, *Perfect Lives.*
GABRIELA AVIGUR-ROTEM, *Heatwave and Crazy Birds.*
HEIMRAD BÄCKER, *transcript.*
DJUNA BARNES, *Ladies Almanack.*
  Ryder.
JOHN BARTH, *LETTERS.*
  Sabbatical.
DONALD BARTHELME, *The King.*
  Paradise.
SVETISLAV BASARA, *Chinese Letter.*
RENÉ BELLETTO, *Dying.*
MARK BINELLI, *Sacco and Vanzetti Must Die!*
ANDREI BITOV, *Pushkin House.*
ANDREJ BLATNIK, *You Do Understand.*
LOUIS PAUL BOON, *Chapel Road.*
  My Little War.
  Summer in Termuren.
ROGER BOYLAN, *Killoyle.*
IGNÁCIO DE LOYOLA BRANDÃO,
  Anonymous Celebrity.
  The Good-Bye Angel.
  Teeth under the Sun.
  Zero.
BONNIE BREMSER,
  Troia: Mexican Memoirs.
CHRISTINE BROOKE-ROSE, *Amalgamemnon.*
BRIGID BROPHY, *In Transit.*
MEREDITH BROSNAN, *Mr. Dynamite.*
GERALD L. BRUNS, *Modern Poetry and the Idea of Language.*
EVGENY BUNIMOVICH AND J. KATES, EDS.,
  Contemporary Russian Poetry: An Anthology.
GABRIELLE BURTON, *Heartbreak Hotel.*
MICHEL BUTOR, *Degrees.*
  Mobile.
  Portrait of the Artist as a Young Ape.
G. CABRERA INFANTE, *Infante's Inferno.*
  Three Trapped Tigers.
JULIETA CAMPOS,
  The Fear of Losing Eurydice.
ANNE CARSON, *Eros the Bittersweet.*
ORLY CASTEL-BLOOM, *Dolly City.*
CAMILO JOSÉ CELA, *Christ versus Arizona.*
  The Family of Pascual Duarte.
  The Hive.
LOUIS-FERDINAND CÉLINE, *Castle to Castle.*
  Conversations with Professor Y.
  London Bridge.

  Normance.
  North.
  Rigadoon.
HUGO CHARTERIS, *The Tide Is Right.*
JEROME CHARYN, *The Tar Baby.*
ERIC CHEVILLARD, *Demolishing Nisard.*
MARC CHOLODENKO, *Mordechai Schamz.*
JOSHUA COHEN, *Witz.*
EMILY HOLMES COLEMAN, *The Shutter of Snow.*
ROBERT COOVER, *A Night at the Movies.*
STANLEY CRAWFORD, *Log of the S.S. The Mrs Unguentine.*
  Some Instructions to My Wife.
ROBERT CREELEY, *Collected Prose.*
RENÉ CREVEL, *Putting My Foot in It.*
RALPH CUSACK, *Cadenza.*
SUSAN DAITCH, *L.C.*
  Storytown.
NICHOLAS DELBANCO,
  The Count of Concord.
  Sherbrookes.
NIGEL DENNIS, *Cards of Identity.*
PETER DIMOCK, *A Short Rhetoric for Leaving the Family.*
ARIEL DORFMAN, *Konfidenz.*
COLEMAN DOWELL,
  The Houses of Children.
  Island People.
  Too Much Flesh and Jabez.
ARKADII DRAGOMOSHCHENKO, *Dust.*
RIKKI DUCORNET, *The Complete Butcher's Tales.*
  The Fountains of Neptune.
  The Jade Cabinet.
  The One Marvelous Thing.
  Phosphor in Dreamland.
  The Stain.
  The Word "Desire."
WILLIAM EASTLAKE, *The Bamboo Bed.*
  Castle Keep.
  Lyric of the Circle Heart.
JEAN ECHENOZ, *Chopin's Move.*
STANLEY ELKIN, *A Bad Man.*
  Boswell: A Modern Comedy.
  Criers and Kibitzers, Kibitzers and Criers.
  The Dick Gibson Show.
  The Franchiser.
  George Mills.
  The Living End.
  The MacGuffin.
  The Magic Kingdom.
  Mrs. Ted Bliss.
  The Rabbi of Lud.
  Van Gogh's Room at Arles.
FRANÇOIS EMMANUEL, *Invitation to a Voyage.*
ANNIE ERNAUX, *Cleaned Out.*
LAUREN FAIRBANKS, *Muzzle Thyself.*
  Sister Carrie.
LESLIE A. FIEDLER, *Love and Death in the American Novel.*
JUAN FILLOY, *Op Oloop.*
GUSTAVE FLAUBERT, *Bouvard and Pécuchet.*
KASS FLEISHER, *Talking out of School.*
FORD MADOX FORD,
  The March of Literature.
JON FOSSE, *Aliss at the Fire.*
  Melancholy.
MAX FRISCH, *I'm Not Stiller.*

SELECTED DALKEY ARCHIVE PAPERBACKS

SELECTED DALKEY ARCHIVE PAPERBACKS

Martereau.
The Planetarium.
ARNO SCHMIDT, *Collected Novellas.*
Collected Stories.
Nobodaddy's Children.
Two Novels.
ASAF SCHUR, *Motti.*
CHRISTINE SCHUTT, *Nightwork.*
GAIL SCOTT, *My Paris.*
DAMION SEARLS, *What We Were Doing and Where We Were Going.*
JUNE AKERS SEESE,
Is This What Other Women Feel Too?
What Waiting Really Means.
BERNARD SHARE, *Inish.*
Transit.
AURELIE SHEEHAN,
Jack Kerouac Is Pregnant.
VIKTOR SHKLOVSKY, *Bowstring.*
Knight's Move.
A Sentimental Journey: Memoirs 1917–1922.
Energy of Delusion: A Book on Plot.
Literature and Cinematography.
Theory of Prose.
Third Factory.
Zoo, or Letters Not about Love.
CLAUDE SIMON, *The Invitation.*
PIERRE SINIAC, *The Collaborators.*
KJERSTI A. SKOMSVOLD, *The Faster I Walk, the Smaller I Am.*
JOSEF ŠKVORECKÝ, *The Engineer of Human Souls.*
GILBERT SORRENTINO,
Aberration of Starlight.
Blue Pastoral.
Crystal Vision.
Imaginative Qualities of Actual Things.
Mulligan Stew.
Pack of Lies.
Red the Fiend.
The Sky Changes.
Something Said.
Splendide-Hôtel.
Steelwork.
Under the Shadow.
W. M. SPACKMAN,
The Complete Fiction.
ANDRZEJ STASIUK, *Dukla.*
Fado.
GERTRUDE STEIN,
Lucy Church Amiably.
The Making of Americans.
A Novel of Thank You.
LARS SVENDSEN, *A Philosophy of Evil.*
PIOTR SZEWC, *Annihilation.*
GONÇALO M. TAVARES, *Jerusalem.*
Joseph Walser's Machine.
Learning to Pray in the Age of Technique.
LUCIAN DAN TEODOROVICI,
Our Circus Presents . . .
NIKANOR TERATOLOGEN, *Assisted Living.*
STEFAN THEMERSON, *Hobson's Island.*
The Mystery of the Sardine.
Tom Harris.
JOHN TOOMEY, *Sleepwalker.*
JEAN-PHILIPPE TOUSSAINT,
The Bathroom.
Camera.
Monsieur.

Running Away.
Self-Portrait Abroad.
Television.
The Truth about Marie.
DUMITRU TSEPENEAG,
Hotel Europa.
The Necessary Marriage.
Pigeon Post.
Vain Art of the Fugue.
ESTHER TUSQUETS, *Stranded.*
DUBRAVKA UGRESIC,
Lend Me Your Character.
Thank You for Not Reading.
MATI UNT, *Brecht at Night.*
Diary of a Blood Donor.
Things in the Night.
ÁLVARO URIBE AND OLIVIA SEARS, EDS.,
Best of Contemporary Mexican Fiction.
ELOY URROZ, *Friction.*
The Obstacles.
LUISA VALENZUELA, *Dark Desires and the Others.*
He Who Searches.
MARJA-LIISA VARTIO,
The Parson's Widow.
PAUL VERHAEGHEN, *Omega Minor.*
AGLAJA VETERANYI, *Why the Child Is Cooking in the Polenta.*
BORIS VIAN, *Heartsnatcher.*
LLORENÇ VILLALONGA, *The Dolls' Room.*
ORNELA VORPSI, *The Country Where No One Ever Dies.*
AUSTRYN WAINHOUSE, *Hedyphagetica.*
PAUL WEST,
Words for a Deaf Daughter & Gala.
CURTIS WHITE,
America's Magic Mountain.
The Idea of Home.
Memories of My Father Watching TV.
Monstrous Possibility: An Invitation to Literary Politics.
Requiem.
DIANE WILLIAMS, *Excitability: Selected Stories.*
Romancer Erector.
DOUGLAS WOOLF, *Wall to Wall.*
Ya! & John-Juan.
JAY WRIGHT, *Polynomials and Pollen.*
The Presentable Art of Reading Absence.
PHILIP WYLIE, *Generation of Vipers.*
MARGUERITE YOUNG, *Angel in the Forest.*
Miss MacIntosh, My Darling.
REYOUNG, *Unbabbling.*
VLADO ŽABOT, *The Succubus.*
ZORAN ŽIVKOVIĆ, *Hidden Camera.*
LOUIS ZUKOFSKY, *Collected Fiction.*
VITOMIL ZUPAN, *Minuet for Guitar.*
SCOTT ZWIREN, *God Head.*

FOR A FULL LIST OF PUBLICATIONS, VISIT:
www.dalkeyarchive.com